FAST MOVES

"Listen, Slocum, I didn't mean no harm!"

"But, mister, I do!" And in a flash he had slammed the man in the belly with the barrel of his six-gun, stepped back, giving him room to double over, then with his left fist smashed him behind the ear. The apologetic victim delivered himself to the hard floor of the Elkhorn saloon, accompanied by the astonished gasps and gaping mouths of the onlookers.

Slocum still had the other two right under his Colt .36 . . .

OTHER BOOKS BY JAKE LOGAN

JAKE LOGAN

A NOOSE FOR SLOCUM

B

BERKLEY BOOKS, NEW YORK

A NOOSE FOR SLOCUM

A Berkley Book / published by arrangement with
the author

PRINTING HISTORY
Berkley edition / October 1990

ISBN: 0-425-12307-3

1

In the soft, singing light of the lengthening evening
the log cabin sure looked inviting. John Slocum had
to check his impulse to just ride on down the long
coulee right now.

He knew better. All his years in the late war and
in the big land west of the Mississippi—not to mention
his Cherokee blood—would never have allowed him
to do such a foolhardy thing. The law of the frontier
was as cold, as sharp to him as the fine edges of a
double-bitted axe; as it was to any man no longer wet
in back of his ears. It took but one bullet to end a
life. And, long as your name was on the bullet, it
didn't matter whose finger was on the trigger.

He sat his little Appaloosa pony, and taking out his
field glasses had a closer look. He was damn tired.
He would have given plenty for a stiff mug of coffee,
some grub, and a solid night's sleep without having
to keep one ear awake against that damn posse. Yet

he felt good—though he wasn't losing any of his caution with the notion that by now he'd lost them.

Studying the cabin, he figured it to be one room—a dirt floor, manure chinking, and the usual share of pack rats to take care of things. Likely a line camp, or possibly one of those cabins you came upon now and again in the mountains, built by nobody knew who but furnishing rest and grub for the traveler—the trapper, cowboy, fence rider, prospector, or owl-hooter, or just plain drifter. Handy.

He favored the cabin's placement, almost hidden in that stand of big timber. There looked to be a horse corral just a few yards away, judging by the thick post and the pole ends attached to it. Because of the trees he couldn't tell the shape or size of the corral or whether there were horses in it.

He knew the logs had to be spruce, since they appeared the most numerous trees around it. And he could see that there was no smoke coming from the chimney. There was no sign of life anywhere. And he was pretty sure there was no horse in the corral.

Slocum was still taking no chances; not after what he'd gone through with that damn posse from Red Lodge. He only hoped now that he was shut of the buggers. He wasn't the man they should have been chasing, but he wasn't about to hang around and argue it.

He waited, watching the blue jay land on the corral post. In another moment it rose and flew toward the north. He didn't have the feeling it had been spooked. Yet he still waited, while the sun dropped closer to the horizon, its light now more intense, turning the long stretch of prairie to the color of rust, all the way up to the edges of the big timber.

The Appaloosa shook his head at a couple of deerflies, one of whom landed on the back of Slocum's bare hand. But Slocum didn't move. He knew that the only way to watch anything was to be absolutely still, and so he sat there in his old stock saddle, right through the twilight. Finally, under partial cover of the early night he touched his bootheel to the Appaloosa and they began quartering down the long, wide draw.

As he'd figured, the corral was empty, and there were no signs of fresh horse droppings to indicate recent occupancy. From where he'd been watching earlier he'd not seen a creek, but now he heard it. He drew rein and waited, smelling the crisp, fresh water, so clear, so much a part of the other night smells— the pine, spruce, his own horse, and the soft, easy odor of saddle leather.

He had dismounted now and placed his hand over his mount's muzzle so that he couldn't whicker if there was another horse about. But there was nothing.

Only the early night mantling himself and the Appaloosa, hiding them and the land around them; though at the same time, because of the hiding from the eyes, both the man's ears and the horse's were sharper, the sense of smell keener. Thus the advantage of night, Slocum reflected. Blinding a man's sight, it opened his sensitivity to sound, to smell, and to the changing currents of air.

It was through this sensitivity—his Cherokee blood perhaps—that he had been saved more than a few times during the recent war, not forgetting the frontier following Appomattox.

He listened, his hand close to the Appaloosa's muzzle. And then he heard the jingle of a horse's bit, very faintly, but strong enough for him to put his hand back on his pony's nostrils. At the same time his other hand slicked the Colt out of its smooth holster. In the next moment he groundhitched the horse and slipped deeper into the trees. And was brought up short by something hanging from the branch of a big cottonwood.

He knew it had to be a body. The horse was standing a few yards away, still saddled; simply standing there patiently, the way horses do.

It took him an instant to see that the man had his hands tied behind his back, that he hadn't been hanging long, but that nevertheless he was dead. Slocum cut him down but refrained from striking a light. He wasn't so sure now about the cabin. He waited, listening.

The sky was now spangled with stars, allowing good visibility, though not only for himself but for anyone else who might happen to be about. He felt the man's hands, went through his empty pockets, rolled him over to look at his face, the outlines of which he could see, but not the details. He appeared young, and judging by the feel of his hands he wasn't a cowboy, nor a farmer. A night rider? In any case he'd been the receiver of an especially vicious form of hanging. Slocum read the signs as he studied the ground, then checked the man's horse, his saddle, his empty rifle scabbard, and then again what he could of the ground beneath the hanging tree. The horse had stood there a while—there was a neat pile of droppings—while the rider struggled to free himself, but painfully careful not to cause the horse to move so that he would be jerked out of the saddle, to be left hanging at the end of the lariat rope, slowly choking to death.

Slocum had checked to see that the victim's neck hadn't been broken as it would have been in a normal hanging. No, for that would have been a swift death. Waiting in his saddle for his horse to move had to be an exquisite torture. Vigilantes? No matter. It would have been a real tough bunch of hardcases to pull a job like that. Looking down at the dead man Slocum felt pulled right into his best attention. The killers might not be very far away. And there was still the cabin.

He had been squatting by the body and now he started to rise, but stopped, and reaching down felt around the man's neck. He didn't want to strike a light. Instead he felt the knot very carefully, at the same time that his ears were keening toward the cabin, the surrounding trees. It was a regular manila lariat rope, the kind any cowboy packed on his saddle, but the knot that made the loop was different; it wasn't a loop that had been built for roping as in a cowhand's lariat. Nor was it a hangman's knot. The rope had been simply knotted around the man's neck with a square knot and two half hitches.

Slocum stood up. Not much that he could make of that, so he simply let it find its own place in his investigation, and now turned his attention toward the cabin.

There was no light showing, no smell of smoke, no sound. Carefully he picked his way along the edge of the timber, and then, deciding on the shortest exposed distance between the trees and the cabin, he crouched low and with his gun in his hand ran swiftly across the open space, pulling up at a corner of the building.

As he stood there listening, something was calling him from the edge of his mind. Something. Something that was out of order, fleetingly noticed as he'd raced across the open space.

A smell? A sound? Something snatched from the side of his eye? And he recalled how he had almost tripped at a certain place, or rather his foot had stepped into a hole. Or—a rut? His eyes swept the clearing. No sign of any wagon. His eyes went soft as he tried for better vision now. But there was nothing. He could find nothing there that would support his suspicion of something more.

It didn't take him long to check the cabin. It was as he'd suspected: one room, dirt floor, a potbelly stove—cold—with a decent supply of firewood, including pitch, and an axe handy for the traveler to replenish the stack. There were three windows, one with cracked glass, one with butcher paper, and the third with both. There was a fair supply of canned goods, plus salt and flour, the makings for biscuits; and there was coffee, sugar. No booze. Evidently the traveler brought his own and departed with same.

With the fire going in the jumbo stove, and with coffee aboard while he rustled some grub, Slocum began to feel better. He'd been on the go ever since Red Lodge, and he was tired, even some saddle sore where he'd been nicked on the inside of his calf by a bullet in the fracas back at the Good Time Saloon. It hadn't felt exactly good rubbing against his stirrup strap. But he was pretty sure he'd shaken the posse.

Having been at that particular moment the only stranger in town had had its usual disadvantage; suspicion more sooner than later found you when trouble was about. Nor was it unlikely, Slocum knew from long experience, that he could have been set up as scapegoat by the real culprit. In any case, he was damn well shut of that action; and glad of it.

He had picketed the Appaloosa rather than letting

him loose in the corral. Anyone coming by would be bound to check the corral, but might not see the horse on the other side of the creek, fairly well hidden behind the willows.

He decided that there was no sense in trying to do anything with the body of the hanged man. Not till daylight at any rate, when he would see better. He had already gone through his pockets, finding nothing that would identify him. Then he'd hidden the body in underbrush, a fair distance from the scene of the lynching. Finally he'd wiped out all sign of his or the Appaloosa's presence. For anyone happening to come by the cabin now he was only a drifter passing through who'd stopped over for a rest and grub, and who'd leave the place in the condition—or better—in which he'd found it.

He baked biscuits, making extra for his next meal on the trail, and then he built himself a smoke and settled down with his second mug of coffee.

It was spring and getting close to roundup time. Slocum figured he'd head west and south to the Sweetwater and sign on for whatever job might be open— roping, branding, or just calf busting; he could do it all, well enough to be considered a top hand. He had never worried about catching on someplace when he needed to collect a little pay. He could bust horses with the best of the bronc stompers, and he could trap and guide, and he'd been a scout more times than he could remember.

By the time he finished his second mug of coffee he'd decided to throw his bedroll outside the cabin, over where the Appaloosa was picketed. He just had a feeling, and he was a man who responded to such.

But even as he stripped his smoke, deciding on where to bed down, he heard the horses. They were coming in fast, like they meant it. He knew it couldn't be the Red Lodge posse; not that quickly, knowing too how well he'd covered his backtrail. No time to douse the coal oil lamp, and anyway under the circumstances it was wiser to play it innocent. He had nothing to do with that dead man; he didn't even know that he existed.

Slocum simply built himself another smoke, waiting right where he was, listening carefully to the men and horses who were taking no pains to hide their arrival. Cowhands? Could be the cabin was used as a line camp. On the other hand, it could be trouble. There was something tense, nervous in the sound of their laughter, cursing, their tempo. And when the door burst open he knew he was right.

He had opened the flap of his cross-draw holster and as the three entered, he was ready. And they saw he was ready.

"Well, lookee here!"

The speaker was big, tall, wide, and thick; a tree. And Slocum could see he was agile. But he was obviously sensible too. He didn't reach for his gun.

"Want me to pop him, Dusty?" said the man beside him. He was carrying a Springfield in one hand, but he was making a fist.

The man called Dusty suddenly chuckled. "He's too fast for you, Jake. Drop it." Dusty's eyes still held Slocum. They were crinkled at the corners. And in spite of the situation, Slocum had a sudden feeling of the big man's good humor. He could see they'd been drinking some.

The third of the trio was smaller and a good bit younger than his two companions; almost a kid with a battered derby hat cocked on his head.

"The man looks fast," the man named Jake said,

his words whistling past his spaced teeth.

"But is he fast as he looks?" the kid wearing the battered derby said.

"They is a way to find out," said the one named Jake, who was midsize between his two companions. "I kin take him, Dust. We dunno who the hell he is and what's he doin' here."

Dusty was still smiling. "Leave it, boys. We be just dropping in," he added, now addressing Slocum, who hadn't relaxed his attention for a second. "So, sir, just unlax a spell." But Slocum was still not letting go of it.

"This here cabin's real cozy-like," the big man said. "Mind if we stop a spell?"

"Make yerselves to home," Slocum said. Yet he still didn't drop it.

Dusty chuckled. It sounded like gravel being dumped out of a wagon box. "See what I mean, brothers? This man is nobody to prod. He is way ahead of little old us." And he stepped further into the room. "Dusty Kitchen's the name. An' this here bigmouth is brother Jake, and this skinny little feller is brother Sonny. We are plumb tuckered and need to rest our heads a spell, providin' you don't mind sharin' this friendly mountain hostel with us."

The smile was all over his face now. Slocum found it almost contagious, but he held a straight face as he said, "Good enough. Name here is Slocum."

Sonny Kitchen now turned on his heel and started to the door.

"Sonny, you tend the hosses, an' I'll just see if we got us some juice in this possibles bag."

"What did you think I was gonna do?" Sonny came back sharp. "Go take a piss or somethin'?"

To which his big brother chuckled, and began taking off his mackinaw coat. He was huge, with hands like slabs of wood. Slocum suddenly thought of a grizzly he'd once had to confront.

Jake Kitchen had leaned his rifle against the log wall nearest him and was unbuttoning his coat. "Didn't figger on company," he said, looking directly at Slocum. And then, over his shoulder to Dusty, who was going through his possibles bag, "He look like a regulator to you, Dust?"

"Could be," Dusty said, without looking up from the bottle of whiskey he had extracted from his bag. "Thing is, he don't smell like one. And it's the stink that counts." And both dropped a wry chuckle at that.

Slocum was still on his guard, wondering if these three had done the lynching and had ridden back perhaps to check on it. But it was a fleeting thought. They were clearly not the kind who would hang a man like that. And what would anyone be checking on at such a time anyway? The man was dead. Any information his killers might have wanted from him was out of the question now. Besides, these men here had to be cowhands.

"Jake, give Sonny a hand and take a look about. I heerd a hoss when we rode in. That yours?" Dusty Kitchen asked suddenly, cocking his head at Slocum.

Slocum threw his thumb over his shoulder. "He's picketed." He wondered immediately about the horse that had belonged to the hanged man. He'd simply let him be; and if anyone came across the animal he would know nothing about it.

Kitchen was watching him. "I'll drink to you tellin' us the straight of things, mister. Just remember me an' my brothers gets itchy sometimes. Sometimes a man gets a feather up his ass and who knows what the hell kin happen then!" And he burst into a great laugh as brother Jake with a big grin on his face opened the door of the cabin and stepped outside.

Slocum nodded. The picture had cleared now. Obviously the boys were on the run. Jake had mentioned regulators; likely working for some big stockgrowers Which meant somebody might be along any minute.

Dusty Kitchen's eyes were grinning now, but not the rest of his face. "That is correct, mister. I am reading it that way too. But we gived 'em the slip. And . . ." His hand dropped to his waist, inches from the big carved wooden grip of his six-gun.

"I hope so," Slocum said as he slipped his fingers along the line of his gun belt and then let his hand move slowly down.

"I got no grind with you, mister."

"Nor me with you, Kitchen. I am not the law. And I don't give a damn what your business is."

"'Ceptin' they is three of us, Slocum. We could easy kill you."

"You could maybe kill me," Slocum said. "But you know same as me it wouldn't be easy."

And in that second he had stepped away from the line of the door, ducked, and had the six-gun in his hand. "Freeze!" His one word cut like a bullet into the room. "Tell your brothers to come on in. Unless you don't mind my finger on this trigger. See, Kitchen, I can be itchy too."

Dusty Kitchen was holding his hands well away from his sides, still smiling. "Good enough," he said.

Slocum said, "We'll leave it then."

And the cabin relaxed perceptibly.

"We'll have us a drink on that," Kitchen said, nodding at Jake and Sonny as the door of the cabin opened and they entered carefully.

The bottle was passed and each took a generous

swig. Slocum was glad to have a drink, even though it did taste like Indian River whiskey.

"Tastes like Injun River, don't it?" Dusty said as he saw Slocum wince.

Slocum managed a grin. "Hooves, snake piss, and all," he said. "Not to mention the strychnine for a good bead."

And they all had a laugh at that.

2

The five windburned men had been riding long and
camping short for more days than they cared to think
about. It had been tough going from Laramie where
they'd broken out, overpowering two of the guards,
finding horses, and then heading north. All the way
to Landusky and the Kid.

But the Kid hadn't been where they'd thought and
so they'd camped in the canyon where, two years
earlier, they'd run in fifty head of the Double Box
herd and started changing brands. The Kid had run
that operation. And it had gone off slicker than milk
through a tin horn. The Kid knew every angle. And
he sure knew what he was doing then: building up a
new herd of five hundred head with his own running
iron brand. After, it had been simple enough driving
those beeves north to Moon Basin and selling them
for a nifty profit. Ah, the Kid was smart!

He wasn't only smart, he was tough as whang

leather and faster'n a piss-ant in heat with that gun he packed in that fancy tooled holster. Not a man to argue.

Except on the next time around something had gone wrong, and the five—Collie, Heavy Bill Hames, Duke, Shadow Boy, and Smitty—had suddenly run into not just a posse of outraged citizens (as a consequence of a couple of other depredations on their part in town) but at the same time the fury of a much more powerful force; the stockgrowers whose stock they had been so rapidly acquiring over the past couple of years. Only the Kid managed to escape the devastating confrontation with the law. In the band of twelve, six had been cut down forever, only the present five surviving sufficiently to be sent to Laramie for their wicked endeavors. The Kid had vanished. Later, it became painfully clear to the imprisoned survivors that he had ratted on them.

But prison was not to their liking and at the earliest opportunity they had broken out. Now, having reached their first destination—Landusky—they had ridden in, on the lookout for the Kid. It had been quite a shenanigans, as Collie, their leader, put it. They hadn't found the Kid, but they'd sure enough found their old friend—Trouble. Even now, camped miles from Landusky and free of any pursuit, they marveled at how they'd gotten away, how they'd found the Kid's brother and what happened.

They sat now around their campfire enjoying the fruits of their adventure. For they were not only free men again, they had evened it some with the Kid— not all the way, but a good bit—and had not so incidentally pulled in a neat packet of bills and coin to boot by holding up a Wells Fargo stage.

"That kid brother sonofabitch sure ain't gonna argue a thing again,'' Collie was saying for maybe the tenth time as he poked at the fire with the old running iron. He was a dumpy, powerful-looking man with a thick beard.

His four companions chuckled, and passed the bottle. "For sure not, after gettin' his neck to part company with his ass, Collie boy,'' said Heavy Bill Hames, his thick jowls shaking like jelly as he chuckled.

That opened it again, how it had all happened. When they'd ridden into town looking for the Kid. Only, not a sign of him, so they'd found a place to wet their dry.

The proprietor of the establishment—a combination clothing store and saloon—had set them right off by the slick way he handled his crutch, being a one-legged man. The crutch happened to be a shotgun, and all five of the boys realized right off that the owner of same knew how to use it.

His name was Luther Bones and he didn't seem at all put out by the five lusty men who had taken over his store and saloon. They were spending money and that was the main point. Landusky consisted of gold miners mostly, with a number of cowboys from the ranches out on the prairie. And upon these the road agents preyed.

The five had downed a few when a big, broad-shouldered, and powerfully-built man swung open the door of the saloon-store, swung it wide, letting it bang against the wall of the building, and strode in as if he either owned the place or else didn't give a damn who did.

Luther Bones greeted the man respectfully, leaning heavily on his shotgun-crutch. "Mornin', Miles, how you be this fine day?''

It was just then, as the boys recalled it at their campfire retelling, that Duke had turned to Shadow Boy and said, "Fer Chrissakes, stop staring. Makes some people mad. For sure he don't look like he's anybody's sweetheart."

"Man's got a face like that," Shadow Boy had answered, "he's gotta expect to be stared at." And he kept his eyes right where they had been.

Duke looked away, not wanting trouble, and moved toward a table carrying his drink. "Let's sit a spell," he said.

Miles Landusky, for whom the town was named, did indeed have a face that made even strong men shudder. Part of his nose was missing, and one eye stared sideways at the world. There was a long scar that ran from his ear down inside his shirt and out of sight.

The story was that some years back he'd been an express guard on the railroad and when a gang boarded and blew the safe with dynamite he'd been standing too close. Following his recovery—which had been slow—he had vowed eternal hatred on gunslingers, road agents, and all assorted crooks, plus gamblers, con men, indeed anyone and everyone of dubious background and existence. But the story had further overtones. It ran that following the explosion, some railroad men had loaded Landusky onto a horse and set out to find a doctor. But the wound bothered him so much that in a fit of rage he yanked out a part of his jawbone, along with a few teeth, and threw it away.

At some point now Heavy Bill Hames leaned forward and said, "I have heard of this feller." He hissed the words, leaning hard on the rickety table.

All of them were now feeling the frightful whiskey—trail stuff, "fit for greasing a wheel hub maybe but naught else," Smitty, the least talkative of the quintet, put it. Then, probably the rotgut loosening his tongue, he added, nodding toward the man with the ghastly face, " 'pears to be the big pisser around this country."

"How you figger that?" Heavy Bill asked.

"I heerd it."

"Yore ass is suckin' wind."

"Lonnie the breed, he told it; down to Lander's outfit; he told it," Smitty insisted. "I remember that n-name," he said, his excitement giving rein to his occasional stammer.

"Told you what," mumbled Collie, who was feeling instant retaliation from the terrible booze.

"I'm tellin' ya!" Smitty had suddenly begun to shake. It invariably upset him to be doubted. "God dammit, I am tellin' you what Lonnie Gripp tolt me— this feller owns everything from hell to breakfast in this here country. He got the town named after him and there ain't a one can sa-s-s-say shit without axin' him, him! Shit, he runs a newspaper—somethin'."

"Who?" Collie mumbled.

"That ugly sonofabitch yonder, G-God d-dammit, with that f-face, face lookin' uglier'n a Texan's asshole!"

Suddenly the big man, who hadn't been paying much attention to the conversation, was standing right behind Smitty and had grabbed him by the collar at the back of his neck, lifted him to his feet, and, gripping him by the seat of his pants, had rammed him right across the floor, through the door, and thrown him into the street. The door hadn't stopped swinging before he was back, six-gun in hand, his face even uglier than before.

Meanwhile, the one-legged proprietor had the remaining four covered with his shotgun; standing on one leg, needless to say.

"Hold it, Mister Landusky! I got 'em covered. You buzzards is under arrest! Mister Landusky, I don't want no killing in this here establishment; but seein' as how I be the law in Landusky, even though the place is named for yerself, I am runnin' this here show, and if a one of them buzzards makes a funny move I will ventilate him with these here blue whistlers, from the ankles all the way up to his dimwit head!"

Now, recounting the hilarious tale to themselves for maybe the third or fourth time since their abrupt departure from the little saloon outside town, the five fell again into delirious laughter over the whole event. But the best had been yet to come, they'd soon discovered. For while they had not found the Kid in Landusky, they had stumbled upon someone even better. By then, nearly riotous with the amount and foul quality of the whiskey they had consumed, they could hardly believe it when they were told at the Best Chance Saloon that the Kid's younger brother was right upstairs enjoying the merchandise. What an opportunity! The brother had tried in vain to defend himself when Smitty and Collie pulled him off his partner, rushed him downstairs, and, having knocked him cold with the barrel of a .45, tied him to a nifty little buckskin they just happened to find at the hitch rack. It had been necessary to shoot their way out of town.

Eluding pursuit, they had finally decided to pitch camp and had forthwith hanged their prisoner. With the "Message to the Kid," as Collie, the least illiterate, had written it, pinned to his coat.

"There won't be no mistakin' what he got hanged fer! Let his goddam brother get it now for turnin' us in!" was how one of the five had said it.

And when Smitty, slower than his companions in the ways of criminal comprehension, had questioned the event, pointing out that now the Kid would really, really be mad, Heavy Hames had informed him that that was the best part of the plan. They would be ready for him.

"That's it, dumbbell. He'll come lookin' for us, and we will be waiting!"

Smitty took a while to get it, while his companions waited in exquisite anticipation, and as the light dawned in his dull eyes, the quintet broke into uncontrollable laughter.

After a while Duke said, "I still think we shoulda took that neat little buckskin horse with us."

"Then how the hell would we of hung the sonofabitch?" Smitty wanted to know.

"We could of hung him regular," Duke said. "Then we'd of had us that neat little pony."

"For Chrissakes!" Heavy Bill Hames exploded. "You want folks figurin' us for a bunch of goddam rustlers?"

At the cabin, the evening passed amicably while Slocum handled his booze with care. His companions, on the other hand, enjoyed themselves nobly as they addressed a brace of bottles of trail whiskey. Slocum kept up with them, as they insisted, but by handling his drinking in a certain way he was able to remain sober. At the same time he was not too sure that the others—especially big Dusty—weren't maybe doing the same. The evening was friendly, but careful. Dusty Kitchen and Jake, too, delighted in telling stories, and brother Sonny delighted in listening. After a while, Slocum decided that in fact Dusty was watching himself but the two brothers were not.

It was Sonny who finally gave the game away. His face had suddenly turned vacant, his eyes were bleary, and his mouth hung loosely open. But the verifying touch was the look of severity on brother Dusty's face when he snapped out: "Sonny, you got yourself a snootful, now that's enough."

To his surprise Slocum saw the tears start out of Sonny's eyes and streak down his thin cheeks.

"Fuckin' baby," snarled Jake, at which point he rolled over from his cross-legged position on his bedroll and collapsed into a raucous snoring.

"I'd say you boys were pretty tired," Slocum said, friendly.

"You mindin' our business, mister, or yer own?" Dusty Kitchen said, his voice prickly. Yet, there didn't seem much anger in him, Slocum noted. He could see that Dusty had been trying to hold his drink, but he had put down a good amount, and while he certainly wasn't in a condition to match Sonny's or Jake's, he was pretty wiped out.

"I mind nothing but my own business," Slocum said. "I don't know where you come from and I don't know where you're going, and I don't care."

Jake was still passed out, his snores now joined by brother Sonny's.

"Good enough," Dusty Kitchen said. "Good enough." He winked one eye slowly at Slocum. "You never seen us, mister. Right?"

"Seen who?"

Slocum was beginning to get a new picture of the three brothers. It was clear now that they weren't road agents, horse thieves, or killers, but they were ob-

viously in some kind of trouble. He decided to take
a chance.

"You boys looking for Texas?" he asked quietly,
his tone friendly. He was referring to the accepted
expression "GTT"—Gone to Texas—which covered
anyone bent on putting distance between himself and
any person or persons who might show a certain curiosity about his business. This could mean the law,
or stock detectives, or simply gunmen.

Dusty's thick lids closed over his eyes as he fought
sleep.

"You be mighty inquis . . ." he started to say, but
couldn't finish the word.

"I mind my own business," Slocum said, "and I
keep my nose clean. At the same time, I don't aim
to get myself in a corner on account of three fellers
maybe running ahead of the law or some fellers with
hot guns, and I might find myself in the same bullet-
and-rope party." And he stood up.

"Where you goin'?"

"I got my bedding outside."

"Outside? What the hell fer? You crazy—when
you could be in here?"

"I see you fellers don't know the first thing about
avoiding the law," Slocum said as he heard Jake stir
behind him, and saw Dusty's hand inch toward his
gun. "And that is, that right now you're a sitting target
if you've got a posse on your tail."

"You 'pear to know a good lot about the law,
mister," Jake said from behind him. He was wide
awake again.

But Slocum wasn't worried. He had their number
now. They were clearly cowhands, or maybe they ran
a small outfit, and something had just gone wrong.
But he couldn't peg them as killers.

He sat down again with the table between himself and Dusty Kitchen. Slocum's hands were in his lap, out of sight.

"We could plug you right now, mister; you better watch yerself." But Dusty's threat was like a small boy's; sulky, taunting but without the tone of conviction that would have warned Slocum.

Slocum was smiling as he said, "And I kin shoot your guts all over that log wall before that," and he leaned forward threateningly, his body almost touching the edge of the table. The gesture was quite clear to Dusty Kitchen; that the smiling, easygoing man opposite him had a gun beneath the table.

"No offence, mister. So take it slow. I was just talkin'."

"Maybe it's just talk, but talk about something different," Slocum said. "Talk about me getting shot up always makes me jittery."

He watched the sweat standing out on Dusty Kitchen's forehead.

"Mister, we ain't killers. We done nothing wrong." It was Sonny's voice unexpectedly cutting in on the tableau.

"Jesus, Sonny," said Jake. "Jesus." But the words were mostly a muttering.

Slocum could hear Sonny's breathing behind him.

"Do you be with that sonofabitch McGann and his bunch?" Sonny suddenly asked.

"Sonny!" Dusty Kitchen's voice was filled with warning.

"Never heard of the gent," Slocum said. "He after you fellers?"

"Slocum, I do believe we could talk, but I would feel a good mite better if you'd take that gun off me." And Dusty Kitchen nodded at the tabletop, about the area where he figured Slocum was covering him.

"Sure," said Slocum, and he brought his two empty hands up and laid them on the table in front of him.

"Well, I'll be buggered," said the big man, flushing at the easy way he had been taken.

"Jesus," muttered Jake, his eyes and mouth round with awe. While brother Sonny emitted some inarticulate sound and started to scratch his crotch, even though it didn't itch.

Slocum nodded toward the bottle. "We'll have a round," he said. "Then maybe you boys will want to tell me what's going on. I can see at one look that as far as dealing with law and outlaw you three don't know your ass from a singletree. It's a wonder to me you lasted this long."

At which the three exchanged looks that as far as Slocum could see were looks of either relief or despair. They had obviously been through more than plenty.

But Dusty Kitchen was made of sterner stuff than he had been showing a moment ago. Now, his chin jutted out, he sniffed loudly, he leaned forward with his forearms on the tabletop, clasping and unclasping his hands. He looked John Slocum straight in the eye.

"We bin screwin' up some, I got no doubt, but we ain't dumbbells, Slocum. So you watch what yer sayin' there."

"I always watch what I am saying," Slocum replied, not giving an inch. "And what I am saying is that you fellers look to be on the run. That right?"

Pause, while the three exchanged looks. Then Dusty nodded.

"That is so, but we got a raw deal. We had to run. Hell, three men can't fight off a army!"

"I am not doubting that you are all three loaded with sand and guts, but you're doing some dumb things is what I bin trying to get across to you, if you'd just have the mind to listen."

"Like what?" Jake asked. "What dumb things?"

"Like I told you, staying in this cabin, where you're all in one place. A posse or whatever could catch you here and all they'd have to do was wait till you ran out of food or tried to make a break for it, and they'd pot you like a target shoot."

"We'll throw our bedding outside," Jake said.

"And you put all your horses in the corral. That too. You should have picketed them in separate places. I'd say you were likely good enough hands around a bunch of hosses or cows, but dealing with guns—that's to say, gunmen and the law and owlhooters—you have got a lot to learn."

The three looked thoroughly chastened by the time Slocum had delivered his little speech, but he saw that they were finally listening to him.

"How'd you figure us like that?" Dusty asked.

"Any man's been about could read you right off," Slocum said.

"Shit," Dusty said wearily and looked at each of his brothers in turn. Then he looked back at Slocum. "You a stock detective?"

"I am not."

"Who are you then?" Jake asked.

"I'm a man who lives where he happens to be at, and I don't aim to hang around this place which any minute could be hit by a posse or a gang of owlhooters looking for you gents." And he stood up.

"Where you going?" Dusty Kitchen's voice was brisk with alarm.

"To check my hoss, and my bedding. Then I might

take a look at your backtrail come morning. If I decide to stick around.''

"We have got the law after us," Dusty said. "But we didn't do nothing. But they came at us shooting, an' we had to cut and run.''

"The law?"

"Think it was vigilantes," said Jake, coming in before Dusty could answer. "Got up by Tom Mc-Gann. So we took off; they didn't look to be in the mind for talking.''

"Slocum, what do you think we oughta do?" Dusty asked. "We can't give ourselves up, and if we keep running maybe we got a chance. But I dunno. Maybe we don't have a chance." And he looked away from Slocum's level gaze.

"When and where was the last you saw the vigilante bunch?"

"Down by Berry Creek, near the north fork of the Wood River," Jake said.

"This morning it was," Sonny said, suddenly finding his voice. "Dawn. We seen 'em about a half mile away.''

"They were on your trail, or were they trying to find it?''

"They looked to be trying to find it," Dusty said. "That's how we read them.''

"Do you think they cut your trail?''

"We were real careful. Walked the horses in the creeks, didn't make camp anywheres. Didn't leave any horseshit around, nothing like that. Hell, Slocum, we are cowmen. Maybe we don't know owlhooting and all that, but by God we can shoot straight and we ain't afraid of a bunch of sonofabitch vigilantes or the stockgrowers' lawmen neither for the matter of that!''
It was Dusty Kitchen who delivered this outburst, and

immediately subsided, nodding in full agreement with what he had just said.

There followed a pause while Slocum built a smoke and lighted it, striking the match on the underside of the table.

He kept his eyes on the three brothers. "They had a reason to be chasing you then, at that time?"

"Some men shot up one of the saloons in town, killed a couple of people, took a hostage with 'em, and hightailed it," Dusty said then. "The law, or leastways the angry citizens, decided it was us. Let me tell you, we just made it."

"What town?" Slocum asked. "Near here?"

"Other side of the mountain," Jake Kitchen said. "More'n a day's normal ride. A man could take two days and still wouldn't be dawdling."

"North?"

"And west," said Sonny.

"The town has got the law? A lawman?" Slocum asked.

"Sure has. And he's closer to the big sonofabitch who runs everything—not only in town but in the whole country—than a itch to a scratch," said Dusty.

"Sounds like a good many towns in this here country," Slocum said, lifting his glass from the table. He took a drink.

"Just where do you boys think you're heading?" he said then.

"Thought we'd head for Billy Mountain country. Get ourselves lost for a spell in them box canyons," Jake said. "Though, I dunno. We also got our families back in the valley where we was raising stock. See, they'll like as not come after them." And Jake looked helplessly at his brothers.

Yet Slocum could see that the three, though up

against about as bad as it could be, were still themselves. He liked it. But he still held himself away from it. It wasn't good to get too close, he knew.

He said. "What's the town where you had all the trouble?"

"Landusky," Sonny said. "Named after the sonofabitch what runs the place."

3

She was a big, dark-haired girl in her twenties, with large, calflike brown eyes, an apparently "sweet disposition," and she could read and write. She was also known to be a good rider, handy with a six-shooter, a rope, a running iron. Most important, she was fully appreciated by no less a personage than Miles Landusky, the owner, publisher, editor and chief reporter of the *Rocky Mountain Declaimer,* a thoroughly vigorous organ of news and entertainment that for a number of years had languished under the uninspired hand of a man bearing the name of Philo Blount. Blount was a man of unquestioned honesty, it was said, but questionable intelligence. He knew nothing about bringing out an organ of news that would capture the interest of the extraordinary variety of persons swarming in and out of the Wyoming Territory—looking for gold, land, grazing rights, adventure, and inevitably other people's money. Parsons, miners, prospectors, con men of all capabilities and varieties, drummers, gamblers, gunmen, even shopkeepers, and to be sure those ladies known in the vernacular as cyprians—all thronged in and out of the town, vending and spending, looking for the silver lining, though settling to be sure for the gold.

She was smart. She wasn't the greatest beauty of all time, and she knew it. She was simple, and in her way—that is, within her understood world—she was honest. She had a code. Nobody could understand why she cared for Miles Landusky. To be sure, he was rich, and since he'd taken over the *Rocky Mountain Declaimer* he was powerful; and he was devoted to the big, rangy dark-haired girl with the big hands, big feet, and big bust. But he was the ugliest man anybody had ever seen—anywhere. On the other hand, as some barroom sage opined, gold was not.

Landusky had discovered her doing business over a saloon in a dingy end-of-track town with the appropriate name of Misery. Sampling her wares, he was impressed by the quality and service. He was even more impressed by the fact that she clearly had no reaction whatsoever to his blasted face. She didn't even appear to notice it. And it immediately became clear that Lily, as she called herself, offered him more than what she ordinarily put out to the trade. He felt something extra coming from her. At the same time, Miles Landusky had learned life the hard way; he didn't let himself go soft. He knew such an attitude to be fatal, especially for a man with his face. He was a realist above all.

He was thinking all this as they lay entwined in the big, though lumpy, brass-postered bed in the big house he'd recently built at the north end of town.

"Ah, that was a good one," she said in her slightly Irish accent.

He liked the brogue, even though it now and again reminded him of his mother.

"Glad you liked it," he said gruffly, speaking into her riot of black hair that was tickling his nose. "Remember, there's more where that came from."

Her laughter tinkled into his hairy chest as she drew a leg tighter across his loins. "I'll remember that."

Her leg had now run up against his erection, and in a moment she had straddled him while for his part he took one of her firm, large breasts in his hand and the other in his mouth. Her legs spread wider and she slid down easily onto his probing organ and as it sank into her she moaned.

And now together they began their sinuous dance, as she opened more and more for him. Suddenly he spun her over, as she cried, "Don't take him out!" in gasping alarm, her buttocks pumping without missing a stroke. Then she was on her back with her legs up on his shoulders, his hands gripping her thrashing buttocks as their pace accelerated, and she began to gasp, then squeal and cry out in delirious joy as the bed rocked, groaned, screamed, stumbling on its legs under the lashing of their desire; while himself, his hideous face no longer contorted, but softened and realigned to a different and unknown emotion, so that for that single, endless moment he had even forgotten how he looked; who he was.

Once again they lay side by side. They were both sweating a little. He reached for the bottle.

"Still good?" he said.

She murmured something inarticulate and snuggled closer to him.

He lay there looking at the ceiling. A long moment

passed. He turned and looked at her, but she appeared asleep, though he was sure she wasn't. He lay back. Without realizing what he was doing he ran his middle finger down the length of the scar that went from the side of his face, just in front of his ear, all the way down to within an inch of his belly button. It was a habit that had grown with the arrival of the scar and some unknown need.

"I've got an idea," he said.

His finger probed his belly button.

"Tell me." She spoke with her eyes closed. "I got to get to work in a while."

"I got an idea," he said again.

She rose up on her elbow and looked down at him. And for a moment they were each motionless, the woman leaning on her elbow, looking down at him, the man lying there with his head on the bunched pillow, tracing his finger along the scar that reached down almost to his belly button.

In the early dawn the cabin was filled with the rich aroma of Arbuckle coffee. Slocum had been the first up, and after tending to his Appaloosa, and checking the condition of the Kitchen brothers' mounts, plus whether there appeared any likelihood of immediate visitors to the cabin, he had built a fire and got the coffee going. While the water was boiling he found the necessaries for hotcakes and began heating the iron that was hanging on the wall for just that purpose.

He had slept well, though lightly and he felt refreshed. The question was whether the posse that had been after the Kitchens had given up, or could they be expected? And too, there was the point that he himself was the object of another posse's attention, if indeed they too were still in hot pursuit.

In any case, it was time to move out. He would still head for the Hardwater Basin. Maybe take on something with one of the outfits during roundup. Roundup was a good time to get lost, with everybody's attention on the branding, the weather, and all.

Soon the brothers came in and poured themselves coffee.

"Which way?" Dusty said as they wolfed down hotcakes and more coffee. "I'd say north and west, and then head back. We got to let that posse cool."

"What about the girls?" Jake asked.

His big brother shrugged, looking down at his plate of food. "What kin a man say? The women will be watched. McGann'll be figurin' on us sneaking back for them. So they'll be waiting, the sonsofbitches."

"What women?" Slocum asked.

Dusty Kitchen put down his tools and picked up his coffee mug with one hand while with the other he scratched into his beard. "My wife, Ellie, for one, and Jake's Gretchen; and we got two sisters—Midge and Drusilla. All of us in two cabins on the south fork of the Fingerhorn; plus my two kids."

He seemed suddenly to have lost his appetite, putting his coffee mug back down on the table without having taken a drink. His eyes were bleak as he looked at Slocum.

Jake's jaw jutted out. "They touch a one of them I'll shave their goddam throats!"

Sonny, so obviously the greenest of the three, began to wag his head. "Dunno why it all got started. All happened so fast! There we was minding our own selves and then all at once these buggers started nudgin' us. Finding fault with some stock of ourn over on *their* grazing; then the water, then the fence.

They strung a fucking fence that a herd of goddam
buffalo couldn't bust through. An' by God it ain't
their land to fence! The bastards!''

"They just crowdin' an' crowdin'," Jake said.

"What did you do about it?" Slocum asked.

"Went to talk to McGann. Tom McGann, he's the
big man in the area. Had all the other outfits lined up
with him. The big outfits, that is. I talked with him
and asked what the hell he thought he was doin', and
the bugger says we was on his land in the first place.
That we was trespassin', and that by God come
roundup he don't want to see none of us Kitchens, or
any other squatters—as he calls us—in his sight.
Talked like he was God Almighty himself in person.''

"What did you tell him?''

"Pointed out to him how everybody knowed him
an' the other big outfits was running real big herds
on government land. Not only did they not pay a damn
cent for that rich graze, but the bastards had fenced
off like thousands of acres of public pasturage. The
small outfits like us, with maybe like a hundred head
or so, was being squeezed off from both grass and
water!''

"What about the law?" Slocum asked, though he
knew the answer to that.

"Slocum, you know same as us," said Dusty
Kitchen, his voice rising. "There is just no legal protection for the little men. The big bastards, they got
their association, and you know now they got the
courts right in their pockets so they even ramrodded
a bill through making it legal for them to seize the
stock of anyone who ain't a member of their goddam
association! What you think of that, eh!'' Dusty
Kitchen was almost purple with anger as his tale accelerated in the telling.

"How many other men are there, I mean the small cowmen?" Slocum asked.

"Not enough," said Sonny, suddenly breaking into the conversation. "They got everything, everything. Everything their way!"

"There is five other families," Jake said. "I'd reckon about eight, nine menfolk." And he cut his eye to Dusty for confirmation.

Dusty added up the men on his fingers. "That's it; if you be counting Herman who isn't more than fourteen, more like thirteen I'd reckon." He looked straight at Slocum. "See, we was sort of rawhiding the group—the others—to stand up with us against the big outfits. And I guess that's why they landed on us. Tried to shoot us up two, three times, but got nowhere; on account of we're not so bad shakes when it comes to an up and open fight. But them big men, Tom McGann an' them, and Wilkes and John Stubbins and Eatherly, they fight dirty. And when the big shootout happened in Landusky—I dunno who done it or for why, but it was us got blamed for it, on account of we were ramrodding the other small outfits to stand up and not let those sonsofbitches run all over us. That's how come we got elected." He stopped for breath. "Just in case you was wondering."

"Anyways," Jake said, picking it up. "They was talking lynching, and we figgered it was best to make ourselves scarce."

"Excepting sooner or later we got to go back," snarled Dusty Kitchen, his face contorted suddenly. "I don't see them sonsofbitches layin' anything onto Ellie and the rest less he's figurin' on a hole in his head."

And he glared into the middle distance.

"You're figuring on slipping back then," Slocum said.

"What else can we do? Can't leave the women and kids to the likes of Tom McGann and his bunch."

"You could go to the law, I reckon," Slocum said quietly.

"What law? The law in Landusky is in Miles Landusky's pocket. And that feller is right backing McGann. And McGann, by God, snaps shit for that ugly sonofabitch!

"What about the law at Fort Madison?"

"Madison? That is a distance, Slocum. An' I don't know if—"

But Slocum interrupted him, carrying out his own line of thought. "'Course, if they're after you for shooting up a saloon and killing a couple of people and the army hears that—well, can you prove it wasn't you? I'm saying, can you convince the army—or anybody—that it was not yourselves did it?"

"If anybody'd listen, they'd know—" Dusty started to say, but Slocum cut him off.

"Nobody's going to listen when it's all heated up. Maybe the army would; except that from what you tell me of this McGann feller, he will surely have got to the army and got his story in."

"That's what we know," Dusty said. "We are just pissin' into a hurricane."

"Then there's only one thing to do," Slocum said.

"Which is . . . ?" Jake said the words, his eyebrows high with his question.

Slocum looked at Dusty Kitchen. "I am sure you boys can just about now figure that one out."

"Catch up with them that did it," said Dusty, his voice soft, his eyes hard.

"But what about our wives an' children, and the others . . . ?"

"Our friends," Sonny cut in. "We got friends . . . ."

They were all looking at Slocum, yet Dusty Kitchen's eyes, though still hard, had taken on some other quality; neither soft nor hard in the usual sense of those words, but something much more durable. Slocum had seen that look before in a man's face, though it was rare. He was glad to see it now. And it was clear what the Kitchens were going to do.

"What're we gonna do, Dust?" Sonny asked after another moment.

"Do?" Dusty turned to his young brother. "What the hell d'you think? We're gonna saddle up and ride for home, that's what we're gonna do. We'll make it by nightfall, coming in over the rimrocks, leave our hosses in the little box canyon, and make it in on foot. No moon. It'll be dark enough."

They were already collecting their gear when Dusty turned to Slocum. "Which way you heading, Slocum? If I ain't being too personal."

Slocum was standing right near the door. He had his Winchester in his left hand. The thumb of his other hand was hooked in his gunbelt, close to his six-gun.

"Figured I might take a look at that Landusky place," he said, and his voice was real easy. "I never bin there, and I've always wanted to know what such a place might be like. Know what I mean? The kind of place you never heard of before."

The sun was still washing the horizon as they saddled up.

"Got something I want to show you boys," Slocum said. And he led them to where the hanged man's body was lying under some underbrush and rocks with which he had more or less covered it.

"Know him?"

"Never saw him before," Jake said. "Who is he?"

I don't know. What about the brand on that horse?"

They didn't recognize that either.

"You planning to take him into town, Slocum?"

"I'm thinking he could be the feller that was taken by the gang that hit Landusky."

"I was thinking the same thing," Dusty said, and his brothers nodded in agreement.

"Be risky taking him in," Jake said. "On the other side of it . . . "

"Might be evidence for you boys," Slocum said thoughtfully. "Whoever did it wanted it to be known who he was."

"You mean, leaving his horse there?"

"I do. Plus and besides the fact they wanted to strangle him in that 'specially cute way."

"If you left him here . . ." Jake the words hang.

"He'd be found—least his horse would—and then somebody'd start looking. And you've all left enough sign about that a blind man could cut your trail."

The three gave a short laugh at that.

"Reckon," Dusty said, not able to think of anything else to say, yet feeling the need. Then he said, "'Preciate your help, Slocum."

"I am looking out for myself," Slocum said. He nodded, then canting his head he said, "You boys tie him on that pony for me."

He waited while they did it. Then he said, "I'll follow after a while. I might just check your back-trail." He grinned at their surprise. "Could be somebody might catch up and get the notion I was part of your party. I wouldn't like that."

• • •

"What I'm sayin' is you ought to open your own place." The late-afternoon sunlight came slanting through the window as they sat facing each other at the kitchen table in his house.

They had just dressed, and she had watched him comb his hair carefully in front of the mirror on top of his dresser. Sometimes it fascinated her to watch the care he took with such things as combing his hair, choosing the right shirt. She had never known a man that neat. And she was always touched by the way he did things for her; seeing that she was comfortable, that she wasn't overtired. There was a kind streak in him, she told herself, and wondered if it had anything to do with his face. Once she had wondered where he came from, telling herself he must have been educated, and was maybe even from a rich family back east. But that once had been the only time.

"I don't see myself opening my own place," she said simply. "There's enough business in town. And I'd be competing with the others, I could get myself in trouble."

The brogue was thicker, he noted, and it usually got so whenever the subject of money or her future came up.

"I'm not talking about you working in town," he said. "I want you to move down to the valley, near where I've got my other place."

She looked surprised. And then, with a teasing smile, "Your secret place?"

"What are you talking about?" he said gruffly.

"I know about it, that's all. And I think it's nice."

"You know about it? What? You know what?" He had raised his voice, but it didn't bother her. She was well aware of how defensive he could get regarding his privacy.

"I just know about it."

"Where did you hear that anything was *secret?*"

"Only from you."

"But I never told you anything. You heard nothing from me. Now listen, Lil, I need to know, I demand to know what and where you heard any of this—nonsense! All I ever told you was that I had another place, a cabin."

She was smiling, though trying hard to control the flutter of nerves that had suddenly struck her, afraid that she might have overstepped something.

"I heard it from you, that's who."

"Why, I never told you anything of the kind, dammit! Now Lil, you listen to me . . . !" He waved his hands. "All I told you was I had a place out of town, in Crazy Woman Basin. Nearby, see, a place where I could just go and, well, do what I liked, without having to have a lot of people around."

"I'm sorry but it was in the *way* you said it. I could tell your cabin was something special, and I was glad."

He was silent, collecting himself. It was something special, all right, but he hadn't *told* her that. It was a damn good hideout was what it was. Nobody ever knew he was there. He had told her only in a moment of passion, though he hadn't told her where it was—not exactly. Only, yes—that was it! The time they'd gone riding down by Alder Creek, and he remembered now how she'd asked him how come he was so familiar with the country since he hadn't been in northern Wyoming that long. That was it. She was smart, wasn't she. Damn smart. He would have to be careful. On the other hand . . . Looking at her now, at the slight flush in her young cheeks, he felt his passion stirring.

"Never mind," he said brusquely. "Never mind. It's—it's just—a place. Where I go to rest, to get away from being so damn busy."

"I know. I know, Bunny."

He felt the sudden thrill as she called him the name she used only in bed.

"Why did you want me down there, so you wouldn't have to travel up here?"

"Just as I said. I want you to open a business there. Look, there isn't another girl in the whole region. So you wouldn't have competition. And there's lots of men. There are ranches there, big outfits; the boys are so blamed woman hungry they'd pay just about any price you were of a mind to charge." He reached out and touched her hand. "Listen, I am suggesting you start off by doubling—no tripling—what you get up here!"

He watched her. She pursed her lips, bent her head a little to one side to look down at her hands that were lying together on the table. It was a long, almost a sideways look. He felt something stir inside him, and cautioned himself again to stick to business.

"Would you be there?" she asked, not raising her eyes, but speaking to her hands as it were, which were now clasped together.

He grinned. "I've a secret I'll let you in on. I've opened a little place down there for the boys to make merry. You know, cards, dice, whiskey. Maybe we could work something together."

Suddenly she was laughing. "That'd be great, hon. Just great! I'll see what I can do. The thing is, though, first of all I need a house, or did you figure me working right alongside you?"

"No, no. Not that. We can't even be seen together.

I've told you that before. What I'm saying is that you could start something on your own and steer people to my place; and see, I'll have somebody else running it; and I can reciprocate."

Her mouth dropped open. "You can *what?*"

"I can send you customers from my gambling and saloon parlor."

"Is that what you're going to name it?" She was smiling at him again, and he felt good.

"Not a bad notion, that," he said, and there was a lift in his voice. "By the way . . ." And he reached over and touched her hand.

"By the way what?" she said.

"I just want to check things out before we seal the partnership."

He stood up and drew her to her feet, and slid his arms around her. His erection pushed between her parted legs.

"Do you think it's satisfactory?" she whispered.

"I'm sure it is, lady. But I am also a careful feller and I'd like to make real sure about such a thing. If you catch my drift."

His hands dropped down and lifted her skirt.

"You've got nothing on underneath," he said.

"I could have told you that," she said.

"Then why didn't you?"

"I thought it'd be nice if you found out all by yourself."

"I agree," he said, and he began unbuttoning her dress down the front.

"Let me help you," she said.

There were a lot of buttons, and so he did.

4

The campfire had burned low, but none of the five seemed to feel the chill in the evening air. They had eaten well, beans mostly and sourdough biscuits washed down with ample supplies of whiskey. Now they were drowsy, though still relating to each other the high points of their adventure in the town, and especially the stretching of the Kid's brother.

"I reckon he's bin found by now," Collie was saying.

"You keep sayin' that, Collie, damn you," snapped Duke, "but I dunno about that. Only way anybody'd ever suspicion anything would be they come across that little buckskin horse of his."

"Well, who says nobody's gonna?" Heavy Bill cut in. "By God, we want him found. We want the Kid to know."

"How's he going to know?" Shadow Boy asked, tilting his head back and eyeing into the whisky bottle to make sure it was empty. "Need that other one," he mumbled.

"The Kid can't help knowing. That's why we left his hoss with him, you dumb shit," Smitty said as Shadow Boy picked up the second bottle. "But I am telling you all I am aiming back to Landusky, or whatever the hell the name of that place was. I am gonna even it with that big ugly sonofabitch. I mean— *even it!*" And his voice rose as he grabbed the bottle from Shadow Boy's hand.

"Don't spill, you fuck you!" snapped Shadow Boy, and he made a grab at the bottle.

The result was that some of the precious fluid was indeed spilled and in the next instant Smitty and Shadow Boy were on their knees—too drunk to stand—slugging it out.

"Cut it!" It was Collie with his six-gun covering the two besotted gladiators. "You want the whole country down on us, for Chrissakes!"

He didn't have to urge them. Both fell back, exhausted from their effort, too weak to carry the dispute further.

"We got to get out of this here country," Heavy Bill said. He was sitting cross-legged with his huge hands lying on his knees like a pair of mallets. Heavy Bill had been known to knock a steer down with a single blow of his fist, smashing the beast right behind its ear. No one who had been around Heavy Bill for even a short while doubted the authenticity of that story.

"I aims to even it with that sonofabitch in town," Smitty said, still enraged over the indignity of having been given the bum's rush out of Luther Bones's Clothing Emporium and Drinking Establishment.

But his companions were more concerned with the

event that had followed that episode; the event that took place at The Best Chance, not far outside of town, when to their astonishment and total delight they learned that the Kid's brother was right at that very moment upstairs with a girl named Frannie. In a flash even their desire for gratification of the flesh was driven from them by the appearance of this higher purpose.

It had gone like clockwork. The Kid's younger brother—and none of them knew his name—gave up without resistance. And the boys departed with their hostage in tremendously high spirits, shooting up one end of the town as they went in retaliation for Smitty, which roused an immediate and vigorous posse. But they had a good start, and the hard ride sobered them up so that they didn't make any more mistakes like that one.

Now, reflecting by the dying campfire, it was coming home to them that they had overstepped themselves in their zeal to bring justice to the Kid's brother.

"Smitty, you want to go on back to that town, you go," Collie said. "Anybody else wants to, then go with him. But you do that, you are one stupid sonofabitch."

"Don't call me that, you, you . . ." Smitty, stalled because he couldn't think of anything else to call Collie other than the words they were fighting over, began to choke. *"Aw fuck it!"* he said finally in a loud voice. *"Fuck it!"*

"Look," Collie said. "We got money. We got good horseflesh. We'll get our asses out of the country. That's what we'll do."

The next voice that came into the conversation was cool and fresh as spring water, its lilting cockney accent all too familiar.

"You boys ain't going anywheres exceptin' where I tell yez."

And with one motion all five turned their heads to look in total amazement at the figure standing only a few feet away from them, a shadowy figure because it came from beyond the rim of firelight. But there was no mistaking the voice. There was no mistaking even the vague shape beyond the firelight. And there was for sure no mistaking the menace of that figure.

Smitty's lips started to quiver. Shadow Boy and Duke simply stared with their mouths open. A tic started to beat under Collie's right eye. And Heavy Bill Hames clenched and unclenched his great fists while two drops of sweat appeared on his corrugated forehead.

"I see you assholes are just as dumb as you always was," the voice said. And a cackling laugh burst against their ears. "I dunno that you're worth this load of blue whistlers, you slobs. But I got to tell you something, you shitheads. That feller you shot and hanged . . ."

A sob broke from Smitty, Shadow Boy was staring bug-eyed at nothing at all, while Collie, Duke—who was white as new paint—and Heavy Bill were still as stone.

"That feller you shot and hanged; you couldn't even do that right. That wasn't my brother. I don't have a brother, you clowns. Don't you know I was born a liar? I never told the truth as long as I can remember!" And the voice broke into an almost uncontrollable cackle, raking their nerves to the point of breaking.

"But if it had been . . ." The crash of the shotgun firing its two loads of deadly pellets into the fire tore the tableau apart. Smitty and Duke broke, sobbing. In the next split instant the Kid had dropped the shotgun and stepped in front of them with his two six-guns in his hands.

Swift as silk he tossed them back into their holsters. And without even a thought coming between, he had them in his fists again.

He was chuckling as he stood there; wraithlike, pale with the sneer in his face, his voice, his posture; and with that unbelievable speed and certainty.

"I'd be wasting me bullets if I drilled you." He holstered his guns. "Learned my skill in Whitechapel, not in the bloody West. You Yanks, you're just plain dumb. Didn't I always tell ya?" And his smile was like a gash in a face that was made up.

"I'll be taking the money you kindly collected," he said now. "I'm a little low in dollars and cents."

"Kid . . ." It was Heavy Bill who found his voice.

"Shut up." Suddenly he hunkered down, moving so fast they were again caught in surprise. "I am sparing you a grisly, slow dying on account of I got a job that needs doin'. Got it?"

The relief that swept the group was almost audible. Smitty had finally got hold of himself and had stopped sobbing.

"Good." Collie had tried to say the word, but it came out as a whisper.

"Speak up, Collie. You was always whisperin'. Huh!"

"I said, 'Good.'"

"I heard you. You think I'm deaf?"

Yet there was a big relief. Familiarity had returned. They knew where they were. The Kid was there to do their thinking for them, to tell them what to do, and how.

"What kind of a job, Kid?" Duke managed to ask.

"Taking care of a few things. Some stock. Some folks too, I do believe."

"Good," echoed Heavy Bill.

A silence fell. The Kid squatted there, his pale eyes with the hooded lids—that reminded some people of a snake—regarding calmly the five who were only slightly returned from their paralysis at his explosive appearance in their midst.

Suddenly the Kid spoke. "I hear you was thinkin' I turned you in to the law." He grinned. There was a drop of water at each corner of his mouth.

"No, Kid. We—"

"I did," the Kid said, cutting across Shadow Boy. "I peached on yez. That's a Limey word, 'peached'; it means I told. You want to know why? I will tell you. I was tired of you, and I wanted you out of my sight; plus I seen I couldn't trust you." He paused, and swift as a striking rattler streaked a jet of brown and yellow spittle at something that had moved on the ground near the fire.

"I have got a need for you now. See, with this job of watching some beeves, and maybe some people too. But I want to remind you of one thing, that I believe you all know about. My encounter with Sheriff Jack Jackson."

At mention of Sheriff Jackson a strangled silence fell upon the group. Jackson had been shot by the Kid, but was only wounded, which it turned out had been intentional. The Kid forthwith had tied the sheriff to a corral gate and spent the rest of the day shooting an arm, a leg, an ear, his kneecaps, his hands, using the man as a target. It went on for some hours until the man finally was able to accept his only out. He gave up the ghost.

"Remember?"

They stared at him, with their eyesockets sagging, their mouths open and bone dry.

"I said, do you remember it!" The words came out like a stream of bullets.

They nodded, mumbled.

Another long pause.

The Kid got up, shook each leg. There was the old, familiar innocent smile on his face. He looked like a choirboy.

"There is a small box canyon a mile up from where the Wood River branches. It forks north. A couple hours ride from that town where you did all your shooting. I will see all five of you there. But you take care to get there separate, not all in the bunch. You got it?"

There was nodding, and someone mumbled something.

"I said, did you get it? God dammit!"

"Got it!" said Collie, and his companions followed suit.

And in the next moment the Kid was gone. It was as though he had simply vanished with a wave of some magician's wand. He didn't seem to move; none of the five could have described his departure. But all at once he was no longer there. And only their twisting fear was left to verify for them that the Kid had really, really been amongst them.

"We got to haul ass," somebody said after a long moment.

"There any whiskey left?"

But the bottle was nowhere to be found.

"Shit," said Shadow Boy. "I could of sworn there was some left. I do by God swear now there was a good bit, on account of I was about to take a drink when he suddenly come."

"The Kid must of took it," Heavy Bill said, almost breathing his awe.

"By God, that was sure a low-down rotten, shitty thing to do," Collie said.

"How'n hell can a man trust a man does a dishonest thing like that?" Shadow Boy asked nobody in particular.

Slocum rode carefully after he left the Kitchens, watching his own backtrail, leaving no evidence of his presence when he stopped to water the Appaloosa or to build a low fire for coffee.

He liked the Kitchens all right, but he really didn't know why he was spending time thinking about them. They seemed to be just what they seemed to be: rough, tough cowmen to the core. But there was too a certain innocence about them. He wondered what their women were like. Just as they were parting, Dusty had told him that Ellie, his wife, was expecting again. They already had two. And he knew that Jake's wife had just started her first pregnancy. They were going to need another cabin. They were going to need the wherewithal to bring two more children into the world. But they were facing the big stockgrowers.

It was an old story; probably going on since the beginning of things; the big men against the little. Well, he had been through it too during the Johnson County war when he'd lined up with the small stockmen against the cattle barons who had it all on their side. Except Nate Champion had shown them. And Slocum was glad, proud that he'd been in on it.

Well, there was no need for him to get tied up in this here. He'd just continue on up north. He didn't owe any man, and he didn't want any man owing him.

And so he dropped the whole thing. He let it go right out of his thoughts.

Which was just as well, for it kept his mind clear when the shot rang out and the rifle bullet whistled real damn close to the back of his neck.

In less than a breath he was kicking the Appaloosa into the stand of willows that lined the creek just ahead of him. Another shot followed but went wild. But he was already out of the saddle, pulling his Winchester with him.

Hunkering down low he surveyed the open prairie he'd just ridden over. There was a benchland off to his right, and he figured the shot had come from there. Probably at the base where there was a lot of cover for any bushwhacker. He was in good cover, and with the creek at his back, so he had a line of retreat. Yet he was hoping that the bushwhacker would think he had fled across the creek.

That had been his plan, anyway, in dumping out of his saddle—to let the other man feel he'd ridden to safety, which was what most men would have done. And it was also what most men who were doing the shooting would figure the target would do. All that had flashed through Slocum's mind even as he was doing it; diving out of the saddle to take a position where he'd get whoever followed up on his attempt at killing him.

The sun beat down on his legs mostly; fortunately, the foliage kept it off his back. Still he was damned hot. His forehead was wet. He had removed his Stetson hat and lay absolutely still now in the knitting silence of the hot afternoon. Out of the side of his eye he could see the Appaloosa had stopped under cover and was waiting patiently.

Where was the bushwhacker? He figured that he'd

moved to a fresh position, probably realizing he'd missed. Slocum felt the trigger of the Winchester.

He waited.

Nothing. No movement. No sound. No strange noises from the land or the animals or birds that would have indicated the other man's position. Who could it be? Someone after the Kitchens, figuring he was one of them? Or was it someone who knew him? Maybe the Red Lodge posse? No, that was not likely. They'd have given up by now anyway, even if they didn't have enough sense to add two and two and see that he couldn't possibly be their true quarry.

No, it was something, someone brand new. Either related to the business with the Kitchen boys or else an outrider looking for points with his cattle boss, or maybe some damn gunslinger. Or . . . ?

All at once he saw the foliage at one end of the benchland move, and somebody came out into the glaring sunlight. At the same time he heard a horse give a loud whinny over the same area. The man was small, wearing a white Stetson hat and bib overalls and carrying a rifle. Slocum couldn't see his face, but the build was slight.

And then suddenly to his astonishment he realized it was a woman.

It was a young woman.

He peered closer.

And she was damn good-looking.

She had only just left, slipping out the side door of the office, into the alley where he was sure no one would see her. He didn't particularly like having her visit him here, but then of course there were those moments that would be quite unexpected, and there would be the need. It was risky, and yet at the same time, the risk added spice to the situation; something he'd always savored. He liked risks. By heaven, he'd had to overcome again and again those great odds against him, since the stupid holdup, the disastrous blowing of the express car. And when it worked, when he got away with the risk—which he always did—it left him with that special lift, that inner singing that he treasured. He had proven something. Again!

Now, with her odor still in the office, he sat near the window in his rocking chair—the chair that helped him think—and reviewed his plan. This event—planning, reflecting, and even probing his position in relation to the town, to his future here—was always good. It was as though he was resting from his eternal combat, and could take strength from the realization of his successes. And thinking too of Lily, certainly, to mention his conquests. Damned if she wasn't the best-looking whore in town!

But he had only been there a moment it seemed when there came a loud knock at the front door. He sat up, his eyes sweeping the room, the press, the other desk, the horsehair couch on which they had just done it, the potbellied stove in the center of the room; cold now because there was no need for it. And called out: "Come." And stood, tall, erect, and, he told himself as he caught himself in the mirror standing on the desk, powerful.

It was a lean, sinewy cowman who walked in, with his big Stetson hat on the back of his head, chewing tobacco, and with a gun set easy at his left hip. Tom McGann was a lefty. Left-handed with his gun, which was interesting, because with everything else he was right-handed—roping, drinking, writing.

Miles Landusky had been expecting him, but in the brief moment of solitude following Lil's hurried visit, he had come close to forgetting his important appointment. Not really, of course; he hadn't really forgotten. What had happened, he realized as all this swept through his mind, was simply that he was much more interested in his new business angle with Lil than with the already established connection with McGann. And yet, for sure the McGann connection was vital. And in the next second the humorous thought passed through his mind that, dammit, it was sure a helluva sight more interesting to do business with Lil than with Tom McGann.

"You're early," Landusky said. "Come in." And he smiled inwardly at the disgust on the rancher's face. A man such as McGann, well, you had to hit the sonofabitch first before he hit you. Those damn stockmen thought their asses was gold, that they owned the whole of creation, and they were doing you a favor talking to you.

He grinned, and looked for any sign of reaction in McGann's hawklike face. Hell, the bugger had come to him, had come as he should, asking for favors. The press. No fooling, he had made absolutely the right move in taking over Blount's newspaper.

And as he waved his visitor to a seat, he thought of Phil Blount, saw him, his body riddled with bullets as he lay in his lined box, and the then sheriff had ridden off with his posse all over the country looking for the killer. And he, the man who a young woman had once said was the ugliest man she'd ever seen, whose face almost made her sick, had evened it. Editor, publisher, owner of the liveliest paper in the territory, and even beyond, his words were read, listened to. And people attended to him—Miles Landusky, by God a man with a town named after him. And that—that, by damn, had been a victory! Getting the town's name changed to Landusky. By jingo, when you knew where the body was buried, when you didn't even have to bother to count the money, and when you knew men as he did—to the very core of theirselves—by the Great Horn Spoon and by God too, you could call the turn!

He sat down, reached forward, and opened the bottom drawer of the rolltop desk and brought out a bottle and two glasses. Meanwhile, he was watching his visitor survey the office.

Good! The man was curious, the man was greedy, the man had a weak spot. What more did you need?

"We'll have one," he said now as he poured, as Tom McGann's attention turned swiftly to the bottle.

The publisher and editor of the *Rocky Mountain Declaimer*, "The Newspaper for the People and in the People's Interest," sat back in his chair. He looked down at his hands. These held power; the power of the payoff, of withholding.

"It's a shipment I just got in from Frisco," he said, nodding at his visitor's glass. "I've got a bottle for you to take along with you." How many bodies did he know were buried where!

Yes, indeed, when you knew the man's weakness, then you knew the man. It was a line he'd used only last week in his editorial.

He grinned behind the mask that was his face for the world.

She was young, maybe in her late twenties. But John Slocum couldn't have cared less about her age. She could have been ninety. He wasn't thinking anything at all about her age. She was obviously tall, though now seated in her saddle on the little dappled gray gelding. She wore a trail hat over her wavy brown

hair, the thick bangs of which roofed the bluest eyes
that he had ever seen. The eyes were set at just the
right width—for Slocum's appraisal. They were a
very light blue, and the whites were very white. She
must have looked that way the day she was born, he
was thinking. But the rest of her had obviously been
acquired. Her body was all but invisible inside the
enormous bib overalls and heavy man's shirt. Even
so, it was impossible for her to conceal her excellent
bosom; that is, as far as size and somewhat of the
shape went. Slocum saw enough in fact—the way
those breasts with the hard nipples pushed at the strain-
ing hickory shirt—to fill his imagination with a riot
of desire.

"Is something a trouble, miss?"

She was surprised, and he could tell it was genuine.

"Why, no, my rifle went off when I was almost
knocked off my horse by a big branch. Is that what
you're talking about, sir?"

Her words were delivered with a lilt. He wasn't
sure what sort of accent it was. But it was unique.
And he was immediately taken. It had been a while
since he'd felt that arrow of desire quivering through
him with such intensity. His eyes dropped to her hand.
No ring. Then she had to be somebody's daughter.

"Your rifle," he said, "that is, your bullet didn't
just go off, miss. It came close, too close as far as
I'm looking at it, for someone packing a thirty-four–
forty without knowing how to handle it."

She had started to smile as he began, but then
swiftly changed to a frown as he got to the point.

"I had no intention of hitting you, shooting you,
sir. And I apologize." Her final words were distinctly
cooler than her opening had been.

Slocum didn't know what to say to that. She had

a backbone for sure, but she didn't appear to have any sense of remorse for having come close to shooting him. Well then, she had to be a greener.

"Where are you from, miss?" he said.

"I'm from right here, sir. Where are you from?"

"What do you mean by 'right here'?" he said, starting to feel his irritation rise. She was damn good-looking, all right; but she was one of the snottiest things he'd met in some while.

"I'm from Spruce Valley. Over there." And she pointed toward the mountains in back of him. "And I'm also from right here since this happens to be my father's range. I suppose you know you are trespassing."

It was just at that point that Slocum spotted the three riders coming toward them. They had only at that moment appeared through the trees where the girl had been, and they were coming on fast.

She had turned her head as the sound of the horses' hooves became clear, and now pulled her horse around so that she faced the riders. Slocum had his full attention on them. Yet he was also fully aware of the rest of the landscape to be sure that nobody else was riding in.

"You all right, Miss McGann?" It was the one in the middle who spoke as the three simultaneously pulled their mounts to a stop.

"Of course I'm all right! What is the matter with you men? Do you think I'm some child who can't take care of herself?"

"Your father's orders, miss. And besides, we wuz concerned."

"What orders!"

Slocum watched the blood rush into her face as she snapped at the speaker, a chunky brute who, like his two companions, was well armed with a sidearm plus a Winchester stock sticking out of its scabbard.

"We ain't been following you, miss. It's that your dad said if we noticed you about—just by accident like—then we ought to see if you wuz all right. So when we heard the shot, and then saw you with him, we thought we better have a look-see."

"We wuz riding fence," one of his companions said quickly, which immediately told Slocum that the three had indeed been trailing her, probably on her father's orders. And he could see that the girl knew that too. She was obviously nobody's mark.

"Well, you can thank my father for me. And I am sorry you were troubled; but now you can ride on about your work." Her tone was cold, bordering on hostile, and Slocum saw how it did not please the trio, especially the one in the middle who had done most of the talking.

"Very well, miss," the man said. "If that's the way you see it."

And he saluted one finger against the brim of his Stetson hat and clicked at his bay horse, turning him with a gesture of the rein alongside its neck.

Slocum instantly caught the sneering look that was thrown at him as the man and horse turned.

"Your dad's concerned about the kind of company you keep, I'd say," the man with the sneer said. And he let fly a jet of saliva across his horse's withers, coming within a hairbreadth of Slocum's left boot.

The next instant he was on the ground as Slocum reached over, grabbed him by the collar, and yanked him out of his saddle. In that same breath he had his Colt out and covering the other two riders, as well as the man on the ground.

"Now git. If I ever see either of you three again I might get mad."

The man on the ground was on his feet, his hand hovering.

"Try it," Slocum said.

"There is three of us, mister."

"Try something and there'll be two," Slocum said. "I told you to git."

In the silence that followed their departure, Slocum didn't look at the girl. He kept the Colt in his hand, realizing that any one of them could pick him off with a rifle shot. But knowing too that they would have the girl to contend with when it came to explaining.

"Thank you for defending me," the girl said simply. "My father certainly means well, but I cannot stand being treated like I was ten years old."

"I wasn't defending you," Slocum said. "I don't allow anybody to spit that close to me. It ain't polite."

"I see." And he was caught by the smile she was trying to hide as she looked down at her hands holding the reins on her saddle horn.

Then she said, "My name is Jillie McGann."

"I'm John Slocum."

"I apologize," she said after a short moment when she seemed to be making up her mind. "Those men of my father's—they're rough, and they sometimes get carried away trying to follow his orders."

"You mean, he's got them buffaloed," Slocum said with a wry grin.

"I reckon so. I mean," she went on, "I guess so."

"I have heard that your pa is the big stockman in this country."

"I suppose so. Everywhere you look you see his cattle. I've only been here a short while. I've been living back east; going to college." She smiled sud-

denly, and it hit him like something had squeezed
him. "I am sorry about nearly shooting you."

"Funny thing," Slocum said thoughtfully. "I am
not."

She didn't say anything to that as their horses fell
into alignment with each other.

They were silent for some moments now and Slocum realized that they were heading toward the
McGann spread. More cattle came into view, and he
also spotted a couple of men on horseback, covering
them from the horizon.

"You don't have to ride in with me," she said
then. "I can manage. And thank you."

They had topped the edge of a long draw that swept
down to a large group of cabins and corrals. He could
see activity in the nearest corral, some men were sacking a bronc, getting him ready for breaking. And
outside a long, low barn somebody was shoeing a
horse. He could see the anvil, the fire, and the steam
rising from the bucket of water after the blacksmith
dipped the red-hot shoe in to cool it before placing it
on the horse's hoof for nailing and clinching.

"Good then," he said. And drew rein, turning to
face her.

She was still looking down at the ranch buildings.
"My dad is very—I guess, possessive," she said.
"So, once again excuse the behavior of his men. And
excuse me for being inhospitable and not inviting you
down for a coffee or something. But—things are a
little . . . difficult, I suppose is the right word."

And then suddenly, without even looking at him,
she had lifted her reins, kicked her dappled gray pony,
and started down the long draw to the ranch.

Slocum sat there watching her for a moment. He
knew that he was being watched, and that as soon as

she was out of sight he might likely be in trouble. Yet he waited, wondering if McGann was down there right now. And if he and his men were getting ready to ride against the Kitchens and the rest of the small stockgrowers. Hell, it was as though the Johnson County war had taught the big stockgrowers nothing. He even had the feeling that they were more arrogant than ever. As for the girl, he had felt the rebellion in her, heard it in her voice. And even though she did have her share of arrogance, he saw it as maybe necessary.

As he turned the Appaloosa and started over the top of the draw to head toward Landusky, he realized that he did want to see her again. Jillie, she had said. Nice. He had never known anyone with a name like that.

5

They had talked for more than an hour, and while his visitor stepped outside for a breath of air, the publisher and editor of the *Rocky Mountain Declaimer* remained in his chair idly writing and doodling on his writing pad, which he held against his crossed thigh.

Then, as often happened, his line of thought straightened and he began to write in full sentences.

"It can be said without the slightest argument or equivocation that none of man's machines is more rare or precious in this Great American West than his printing press. It has braved the seas, the rivers, and the floods, and has run the gauntlet of hostile Indians. It has crossed the Great Continent, braced deserts, conquered mountains. It has suffered the depredations, the banditry of those who live in the lowest echelons of skullduggery. And while often threatened with extinction, it has never flinched when the hour of duty called!"

He sat back, rereading it. It was good. There was what might be termed "colorful exaggeration," but the readers liked it. After all, as any newspaperman who was worth a tinker's dam knew, the public—those who were able to read—wanted news. And when there wasn't news of a gold rush, an Indian massacre, or something of equally exciting caliber, then the columns had to be filled with folksy local patter.

He well remembered some of those tasty tales, such as one he had only recently purloined from a rival paper: "When Obediah Foames was shot to death in the doorway of the Long Arm Saloon last Friday night, it is reliably reported that he bled not blood, but 100 percent pure bourbon whiskey. . . ."

His eyes, one of which was so badly damaged he could barely see out of it, went to the ceiling as he reflected on the pleasures and difficulties of journalism.

The back door opened and Tom McGann came back into the cluttered office. The doorway wasn't that low that he had to stoop, yet he did anyway from force of habit; and he lowered his wiry body, which seemed to be all bone and sinew, into the chair he'd only recently vacated.

"We'll start roundup pretty directly," he said, continuing the conversation. "'Bout a week, ten days, I'd hazard. It'll give us a jump on the nesters."

"The Kitchens are not going to be happy with that, are they." Landusky said it as a statement.

"Tough," the rancher said.

Miles Landusky studied him again briefly, sizing the man, and recalling abruptly how only a few years back, he himself had robbed the cattle barons blind.

The thought gave him a great satisfaction whenever he was with McGann.

Those were the good days, riding high with the boys. That had been down in the Panhandle. That had been before he had changed his name to Landusky; before the dynamite. Well, if that goddam thing hadn't done anything else, it had given him a disguise that nobody—not even the smartest Pinkerton or Wells Fargo agent—could crack. Dammit, it had even given him a new voice; and it could be that was the best. Nobody, no one could see even a trace of the great Butch Killigan, former night rider, cattle rustler, horse thief, bank robber, and anything else—even fake lawman—you pick it.

And the cute thing was that the accident—the dynamite—had happened right when the law was getting hot. The terrible thing had turned out to be the saving grace. Yes, and the way he had spread the story around—little pieces here and there—about being an express guard, severely injured while defending the railroad's gold shipment. Luck and genius!

Sitting there now—in his new life, his new adventure—he regarded Tom McGann and decided again that he was useful. Because, sonofabitch though he was, he was straight with his code. Therefore, you could count on him. Of course, himself—Miles Landusky as he had called himself for the past seven years—didn't trust anyone but himself. Never had. Oh, the fools who went around trusting!

And while McGann lighted a cigar, his host continued to reflect on his new role as a valiant frontier editor leading the fight for law and order in the community. Such had been his enterprise and success in combating crime that the citizens of the community in which he had led the way had changed the name of their town to Landusky in his honor. Yes, with a little persuasion here and there to be sure.

As the thought came again to him while watching the cattleman, he almost smiled; though he knew too that with his face, no one really knew whether or not he was in fact smiling. He didn't care. He could deal 'em now from any place in the deck. And he was doing so. It was all right. It was all, all right. And it was especially all right now since he'd heard that the Kid and some of the boys had left Texas and ridden north.

Behind all those scars, those smashed bones, and the agony he had lived, his soul was grinning. It would be real good fun dealing with the Kid again; his former lieutenant; and yes, pupil. The snotty little bastard was giving himself airs now; he'd bet a stack on it. And it would be the acid test, fooling the Kid.

"Then you're ready to go," he said aloud to McGann, who had just sent a perfect blue ring of tobacco smoke toward the ceiling.

"I am. And I am glad—we are all glad—to have you on our side, Landusky. Public opinion is important these days. And when a man, when men have the right on their side, nothing can stop them."

"The West is growing," Landusky said, thinking of his next editorial. "We'll be a state one of these days, not just a territory." And he looked meaningfully at Tom McGann.

"I know you used to be on the town council, Landusky, and I've suggested before that you run for mayor. We need a mayor in this town. I mean, that title is important. And as a fighter for justice and the cleaning up of the outlaws and rustlers and hoss thieves, you'll get all the backing you'd need. I'm saying again, we need a man like yourself holding the reins.''

"I've told you, I'll think about it.'' The words came out carefully, carefully mixed with the right amount of modesty and awe. "I would of course be honored, though again, I in no way seek such a position.''

"I understand.'' McGann took a pull at his drink. "But I happen to know the people will vote for you. You've been off the council for a while—when you retired to give more time to your paper—and now you are seen as a strong, faithful public servant. Plus, the office of mayor will be newly created. It all adds up to just what we need. Landusky, you've got to consider it. The cattlemen are behind you one hundred percent!''

The editor of the *Rocky Mountain Declaimer* put down his glass and leaned forward. It was time to deal one from the middle of the deck.

"Tom,'' he said, leveling his uneven eyes on the cattleman. "I am planning a series of articles on the men who have carved civilization out of this rugged, desperate land. In a word, the cattlemen, the ranchers who have brought us all to our present bounty. And if you agree, I plan to start my series with yourself.''

He watched it hit McGann right in the guts. The surprise, the instant pleasure; then the suspicion, but this was wiped out with the shining picture of himself spread all over the *Declaimer*; all over the West; and maybe even further.

"Landusky, I'm not sure I . . .''

And the man sitting opposite him almost snapped his jaws shut. Anyone who would have been capable of holding his vision long enough on Miles Landusky's face to see behind its hideousness would surely have seen the wolf snapping down on its victim. But men didn't care to look directly into that man's face; and so nobody ever managed to see anything at all of what was really going on there.

And Miles Landusky fully realized this.

After leaving the girl he had ridden east toward the high rimrocks, away from the McGann outfit, away from the big valley and the Kitchens, and even away from his original destination, Landusky. After a good while, when he was satisfied nobody was following him, he cut back, making sure his backtrail was clean now, and rode the rim of the big valley looking down on the Kitchen spread and two other outfits that were among the small stockgrowers who were still standing against Tom McGann.

It was a big area, with good feed and water, and with access to the mountains where the stock could be brought up and left for summer grazing. For some moments he considered riding down to visit the Kitchens, but decided against it. He would visit later. Right now he had much to do in town, seeing what he could find out about the cattlemen, and the fight that was shaping up. For it was plain as a fresh brand on a fresh calf that it had to happen. It was the story all over the West, after all. The big cattlemen and the small. A simple war, enacted again and again. The land stolen from the Indian, and then stolen from each other. Pretty soon, as any man could see, there'd be no more land to steal. Then what? But his thoughts didn't go further than that. Right now he was thinking about the setup in the valley; the explosion that was inevitable, and how he'd seen it before, knew the signs, the sound of it, could as much as smell the trouble coming.

And the girl? Did she wonder? Did a person like

that feel the tension in the air? And if she did, what did it mean to her? Anything?

Now, sure that no one was on his trail, he changed his direction again and turned the Appaloosa toward the south and west, with the long sun slanting across the land, and the air freshening with the coming of the evening, the night, and the following dawn, with the many days and nights coming after in relentless succession.

What was drawing him here? He could have ridden on. It was his way, wasn't it? To ride on. His life, after all, was the life of a drifter. He was a nomad. Like the Indian, the land was his home. He did not see himself ever settling down with, say, a section of land and a handful of cows. Of course, strange things did happen in this world. Only there was so much to see, so many things to do. He wasn't ready to settle down; and maybe he never would be. He had thought he might, after the war when he'd returned to Georgia. But it was spelled right out that it wasn't to be. And he'd headed west; that great endlessly open space that was like the sky; the more you followed it the more there was to follow. And he knew without saying it in words or even seeing it in pictures that it was the only place he wanted, the only way he ever wanted to be.

There was the first hint of the coming dawn in the solemn sky when he sighted the three, four lights far below. He could smell the nearness of rain then as a sudden light wind brought that freshness that an old Indian had once told him was the herald of the creation.

The first spatter of the new rain was touching him as he rode in the rich odor of the wonderful land toward the winking town.

• • •

He was bucktoothed, probably knock-kneed, short.
More boy than man, with pale, watery eyes that
showed a lot of red streaks in with the blue, his voice
was high, whiny. Altogether, he looked rheumy, snot-
nosed, and it was assumed that he enjoyed very bad
habits. Now and again a drop of water would form
on the end of his pinched nose, but he would never
brush it off, leaving it there until it fell of its own
accord. Miles Landusky, back in the days when he
was Butch Killigan, "The Terror of the Plains,"
would say that this showed the Kid was considerate,
allowing the drop of water to live out its existence
without his interference. The Kid did not show such
consideration, however, for his fellow man.

Back in that former time, Butch Killigan had one
good word to say for the Kid; he was "handy." Hell,
hadn't he seen the skinny little sonofabitch stick a
wooden lucifer on a corral post, then pace off, turn
and throw down, and by God light that match? Yes,
the Kid had his uses. And the Kid knew one thing,
and Butch Killigan had made sure he knew it. The
Kid knew that the only man about who wasn't afraid
of him was Butch Killigan. Butch kept the Kid in line.

But then there'd been the Northern Pacific job at
Newcastle. So clearly he remembered it—every detail—at least till the end. Lonesome Lonnie had
lugged the huge side of beef into the express car, and
he had taken it from him and lifted it to the top of
the safe. Then he'd called to Lonesome, "Get me the
stuff . . ." And from outside the express car John Dipper tossed a black bundle of dynamite sticks into Killigan's waiting hands. He'd pushed the dynamite
under the beef then, lit the fuse, and they'd all jumped
off the car, dragging the express guard with them.

Except that something had caught him in the leg and he was down. And in that split instant the explosion cut the night and all he knew then was the terrible searing, never-ending agony.

Butch Killigan, "The Terror of the Plains," died then. The gang had hidden out in the big swamp, but the lawmen soon found them; and except for the Kid, and also except for Butch Killigan, they were all caught or killed. And also excepting John Dipper who miraculously appeared at his side and helped him get away.

For days and nights, for weeks, he was in the shadow of hell. Dip got him to Doc. That faithful man knew his job and stitched him together "So yore old ma wouldn't know you." Butch Killigan recovered, but he had a new face. He would never forget Johnnie Dipper's expression when he first looked at the man he had helped escape from the disastrous holdup. But because of the Dip's horrified expression, which he was unable to hide, Butch Killigan knew what he looked like. And then one day he took hold of himself and asked for a mirror.

Doc and John Dipper were both present when he looked at himself for the first time. He had wanted it that way.

"Sure you're ready?" Doc, a man famous for phlegm and understatement, had asked.

"Give me the mirror."

In retrospect, much later, it had seemed to him that it was harder on the two of them than on himself. They had both stood there by the side of the bed as he lifted the mirror.

He didn't say anything. He handed the mirror back. He'd been in bed a long time. Strangely, he was suddenly remembering his early life back in Massachusetts, wondering if any family was still there. And then he'd thought of school, college. What were they all doing now? His classmates!

He looked up at Johnnie Dipper and Doc. And these "classmates"!

"Doc, I've got money cached. I'll see you're taken care of for the rest of your life. And you too, Dip. But just remember one thing if you want to live to spend that money. Butch Killigan is dead."

"That's what the papers and all been saying," Dipper said. "Like we told you. Dunno how they ever got the notion, but there was such a mess of bodies in that swamp, they somehow got the story like that."

"It's a mystery," Doc said, scratching into his gray mustache with his little finger. "But every paper, and people all over, been saying how the Killigan gang was wiped out and Butch Killigan is dead."

"They got everybody?"

"Near as we can figger. Excepting yours truly," John Dipper said. "But most people didn't know me much."

"You were always a quiet one, Johnnie. It's the best way, I bin thinking. And what about the Kid?"

"The Kid?" Doc's eyebrows lifted in surprise. "Why, there hasn't been a mention of him, has there, Dip?"

"Nothing. Course, the Kid warn't there at Newcastle."

The Dip had moved his head slowly from side to side. He was staring at the man in bed, who now was trying to sit up.

"What is it?" Doc asked.

"Don't you see!" Killigan said. "Fer Christ's sake, that little sonofabitch turned us in! He's disappeared, and he made a deal with the law not to mention him.

You sure they got everybody? The whole bunch?"
He had sunk back into his pillow, exhausted.

"All of them that was there. But remember you
had Collie and them back at the place, back at Star
Trap." Johnnie Dipper had leaned over the man lying
in bed. "You really figger somebody spilled!" John
Dipper was a man with a long face, which now looked
even longer as his jaw dropped open in awe for what
he had just come to realize.

"Fer Chrissakes, Dip, how else can you figger it?
That little sonofabitch wanted to take over, and by
God he did."

Neither Doc nor Dip said anything to that. There
was just nothing to say.

But finally, Dipper did speak. He said, "Butch—"

And suddenly he was looking into the round hole
of the six-shooter that the man in the bed was holding in his hand, the man with the burnt and broken
face, the man who still moved with the speed of a
whip!

"I told you, mister! Butch Killigan is dead. There
is no one alive named Butch Killigan. Remember this,
you little sonofabitch; I have just let you fuck up—
once. That is more than I ever allowed anybody. And
it's the last time—the only time—that you will fuck
up!"

John Dipper was white as paint. He was shaking.
But suddenly there was a glow in his eyes. "I—I got
you. I got ya!" And though the grin on his face was
shaky, it was there.

The gun barrel swung to Doc. Doc's Adam's apple
pumped.

"Funny you mention that name, sir. Far as I hear
tell, that man was killed by the law while holding up
a Northern Pacific express car. Got shot all to hell, I

bin told. I believe he was diagnosed as dead, sir!''

The man lying in the bed had grinned then, and he watched the two faces that were looking down at him. He knew what was going on behind those masks; they were thinking that he was just as ugly grinning as when he was not.

Now, as Miles Landusky sat facing Tom McGann in the office of the *Rocky Mountain Declaimer*, he was wondering what had set him suddenly to thinking of the Kid. Way up here in a new country, with all those years between. To think of the Kid like that and the Northern Pacific at Newcastle . . . and all that had followed.

And he had lived. That was the big thing. God, how he had lived! He knew every day of those years. Every long day and longer night.

So strange, how all that had come back; the memories. Going back to memories of back east, home, college, running away. Throwing his education out the window. And for the excitement!

Now, facing Tom McGann, he understood very well why and how all that past had suddenly come up in his mind. It was a new life, yes; but he had not really forgotten the old. He would never forget Newcastle. He would settle it; and maybe then it would be over.

Funny. Funny too how that man sitting there in front of him, savoring that cigar and that drink, had mentioned how he was going to have to bring in ''extra hands.'' Somehow he had known McGann was going to tell him that.

''You mean guns,'' Landusky had said quietly, feeling the quiet smile playing at his mouth.

The cattleman nodded. ''I mean guns.'' He

shrugged. "Look, those damn outfits been robbing us blind. On top of the fact that they're always trespassin' on my graze, dirtying the water, and just in the goddam way in general!" His voice had risen as he became more wound up. And Miles Landusky found himself nodding silently. He'd heard it all so many times before.

"Hell, they're gettin' to be out-and-out rustlers," McGann said with hardly a pause. "And the law don't want to do anythin' about them." He put down his drink and stood up. "Well, no point cryin' over what's spilt." He sniffed, studied the ash on his cigar, and said, "Got me some good men, it 'pears. And Jug, my foreman, agrees. Hell, Landusky, I don't like hiring hardcases, but so long as they're basically cowmen, I'll go along with the others."

"These men—they're cowmen?"

"They're drovers. Wouldn't of hired 'em otherwise. I spoke with them myself, and with their leader."

"Leader?"

"They had a feller ramrodding them. They tell me they go about looking for work here and there—busting hosses, roundup, branding, working cattle. The usual. I am telling you on account of I want you to know I am sticking with the law. You tell me it's wrong to hire them five, six men and I'll cut 'em right off the payroll."

"I always go by the fact that a man's innocent till somebody proves him guilty."

"Good enough." A grin started across McGann's doughy face.

"And I ain't the law anyway," Landusky said.

"You're more than the law, Landusky. You're that newspaper. And that's what counts; what people get through your paper; here, or anywhere else they're printing news."

"Well, maybe. Maybe so."

They were standing facing each other, playing for an opening, as Landusky put it to himself. And then all at once he knew why he'd been thinking about the Kid.

"Matter of fact, Tom," he said easily, "I already heard you'd hired some new hands."

"News gets around fast, don't it?" And reaching up the rancher scratched deep into his left ear.

"Heard you had some young feller, looked kind of like a runt. Somebody said he put him in mind of Billy Candle."

"Matter of fact, he does. Got teeth that stick out. Not that I ever saw Billy Candle. But I have heerd plenty, like I reckon about everybody has."

"Candle's dead, course," Landusky said conversationally, shoving one hand in his pants pocket to scratch a sudden itch.

"Well, I don't know too much about this young feller, exceptin' he 'pears to be the leader of the five men what my ramrod signed on."

"Tom, I hope you know, and I hope everybody else in this town knows, that while I am newer here than most of you-all who opened up the range, I am still with you. I'm one of you. And I think the support I've been giving you in the *Declaimer* bears witness to that."

"It does, Miles. It does indeed. I know that all the stockgrowers favor what you write in your paper. And I just am wanting to keep on our good relations."

"Likewise."

Suddenly Tom McGann stuck out his hand. "I'd like to shake on that, Landusky."

"Good enough."

The grip was strong. In fact, the rancher was surprised at the power in the newspaper editor's hand; even though he had heard the story of Landusky running one of the five men he'd hired right out of Luther Bones's drinking place. Just like that, quicker'n a rabbit having at it! Well, Landusky, as everybody had been saying, was a good man to be in with. Which was why he'd paid his visit.

And as Tom McGann closed the door of the newspaper office behind him and started down the street, he was thinking. Why not; he, Tom McGann, was a good man to be on the right side of too. And he reckoned that Miles Landusky must have figured it out that way. The man was smart as a whip. Seemed educated, like he'd been to college or something like. The rumor had it he was from back east, but that he was no man to mess with. But God, that face. Somebody said it had been a dynamite explosion in some mine. Well, maybe he'd been a miner before the newspaper. He didn't know. But what he did know was what he'd been telling his fellow stockgrowers for some long while, that a newspaper was a good thing to have on your side in times of trouble—like right now—and especially it was good to have a tough man like Miles Landusky backing your play. By God, they'd run those sonsofbitchin' Kitchens plumb out of the country before the snow started to fall!

6

There wasn't much that could astonish John Slocum, at least as far as his fellow human being was concerned. But the sudden and totally unexpected reappearance of Jillie McGann surely earned his amazement, not to overlook his great delight. Since leaving her earlier in the day he had ridden over to the valley where the Kitchens held sway—at least for the present—and, without riding in to the ranch houses, covered a good bit of the territory, studying the water, the grass, the formation of the land, the fences McGann had strung around them, and he'd made a rough count of the stock. Twice he had spotted lone riders, but not up close, and was fairly sure he hadn't been seen.

He hadn't spotted any of the Kitchens, but did see two of their horses in one of the corrals. He had felt better then, having become at least a little familiar with the run of the land. It was around the middle of the afternoon when he started to head directly toward Landusky.

He'd only made that decision about fifteen minutes ago when there she was, still in the same tight riding britches and silk shirt, her wavy brown hair blowing in the light wind that had suddenly arisen; her light blue eyes brilliant. In fact, it was clear that she was barely controlling an excitement.

"So here you are again!" There was the same lilt in her voice, and the same thrust of her breasts as she sat straight and well in her roping saddle with the low cantle.

"I reckon you can't get shut of me as easy as all that, miss," he said, feeling his senses race as he took in her fantastic figure and the bright shining glance she was holding on him.

They had both reined their mounts and now sat facing each other, their ponies kicking at flies, bridles jingling, while Slocum valiantly tore his eyes from her every other moment to make sure of her backtrail.

"I don't believe I'm being followed this time," she said.

"I don't believe so either. Maybe you scared them off."

"Maybe you did, you mean!" And she tilted her head at him.

He had never seen such blue eyes in his life.

"Actually," she went on, "I think it was a good thing; what happened with those three men. I forget their names. And it doesn't matter. But they are loyal to my father, and do just what he wants; even breathing or not as he might order them."

At which they both laughed.

She went on. "It was good because I had it out

with Dad. Of course, I have it out with Dad just about every day.''

And again they both broke into laughter.

Then, without either of them saying anything, they had started walking their horses side by side, not aiming in any particular direction, but somehow agreeing without saying so that they wanted to get away from the place where they had just met again.

''It seems to me you spend a good deal of time bringing up your paw,'' he said.

''Did you bring up your parents?''she asked. And as she smiled, he caught the dimple in the side of her face. And his breath quickened.

''I had enough trouble bringing up myself,'' he said.

They were near the little creek that he had decided to head for, and without either saying anything they both drew rein. Both horses began immediately to crop the short buffalo grass, their bits jangling, while they now and again shook their heads at the random deerflies.

She was laughing at his remark about bringing up himself, and suddenly she stopped, as though a thought had occurred to her.

''You appear to have something on your mind, Mr. Slocum. Are you worried that maybe those men are following us?''

''No, miss. I'm not.'' And he sat his pony quietly, looking steadily at her until he saw the color rise in her cheeks, and then he looked away. ''Of course, they could like accidentally cut our trail,'' he said. ''Maybe we might move in closer to the creek where it isn't so hot.''

''I think that is a very sensible decision,'' she said, her voice grave. And he cut his eye at her quickly for funning. But she was serious as a sober judge.

There were willows lining the creek, and it was cool in their protection, and also the light wasn't carrying the brilliant directness of the blazing sun.

Without a word Slocum dismounted and stood by his horse while she did the same.

"It's almost like a cave in here," she said.

"I like that name—Jillie."

"The name actually is Gillian."

"That's nice too."

"John's a good name. It suggests honesty and directness and—what? Adventure, I would guess."

He didn't say anything. He was simply standing there taking her in. She had a freshness about her that he hadn't seen in a woman for a while. It seemed to be a freshness of innocence. And yet, at the same time, there was clearly a wisdom about her. Innocence and experience both at the same time, was how he saw it.

"Do you want a drink of water?" she asked, nodding lightly toward the creek.

"I just gave my horse some a while back," he said.

And in the next moment he was beside her, and then she was in his arms.

Neither said a word; there was no need. They stood there, their lips, their mouths taking each other hungrily. While his erection drove hard between her legs, and she offered not the least resistance.

For a moment he drew back to look at her. She was having trouble breathing. Then, without speaking, he led her by the hand to a tree where the ground was soft and more or less even for the area they would need. And he was taking off her clothes, and she his.

It took a while, for they had only four hands, and there was so much to discover and play with.

He had first pulled off her blouse and her breasts seemed to spring into his eager hands. Soft as silk, firm and proud they responded with hardened nipples as he squeezed and stroked. Meanwhile she had reached down and was rubbing the great stick that was pushing his trousers out like a tent.

Then they were pulling off their clothes, and the sun was hot on his back as he laid her down on his shirt and her blouse, totally naked, and mounted her, slipping into her soaking bush as easily as the dawn slipping into the joy of the morning sky.

She had spread herself wide, with her legs now up around his neck, while his hands held her buttocks, and together they began to stroke sinuously, finding the mutual rhythm, or rather letting their bodies find it. The marvelous dance that slowly increased and then became faster; and faster until their bodies were no longer two but one, and they came in an explosion of total ecstasy, their come meeting like two waves sweeping into each other at a time that had not been planned, but that had been inevitable.

He lay in her now as his erection softened, though still remained large, and her buttocks were still, her thighs and legs slipping away from him, though still touching, but no longer thrashing in that superb scissor hold at which he found to his delight she was so expert.

"My God, I needed that," she whispered. She was lying on her back still and he had rolled away to lie beside her. She had addressed her words to the sky, and now she turned her face toward him as he rose up on an elbow and looked down on her.

"Me too," Slocum said.

"You're a wonderful lover."

"You're pretty good too."

But she didn't rise to the teasing. "It's because of

you, what you do to me," she said simply.

"You do some things pretty damn good too," he said. And this time he wasn't teasing.

He lay on his back beside her and they both watched the westering sun as it got closer to the horizon.

"Pretty soon it will be dark," she said after a while.

"Might be fun to try it in the dark," Slocum said, and he felt his erection poke into her hip as he turned toward her.

"Why wait?" And she turned to meet him, reaching down to grasp his big organ and rub it into her fur, then into just the opening of her lips.

"I meant later," he whispered in her ear as he moved into her spread legs. "After this one, I'm talking about the next."

She had guided his organ right in all the way, and he nearly came with her tightness, slipping along his sliding manhood as she rotated her hips and buttocks in the most marvelously slow tempo; just exquisitely right.

This time he flooded her even more, and even felt their come flowing onto his thighs, and then up onto her belly.

They lay together, satiated and benign, their bodies holding an exhausted and still-exquisite joy as the sun reached the horizon.

"I want to take you into my bed," she said.

"I think your dad might have some objection."

"I suppose. But then, of course, you might."

"The only objection I might have would be the sudden arrival of company. I like privacy when I make love."

"But of course. So do I!" She turned toward him. "Why, you didn't think . . . ?"

"Think what?"

"Think that I wanted somebody *watching!*"

"It didn't enter my mind," Slocum said. "But now that you mention it, no—I wouldn't care for that."

"Well, neither would I!" And then she said, "How in the world did we ever get onto such a subject?"

He slipped his arm under her neck and she snuggled close to him, her face feeling his chest.

"I loved it—both times."

Her lips were even hungrier now as he kissed her, and when he embraced her, her belly was like silk against his.

This time they moved more slowly. After all, as he told her at one point, there was no need to hurry. And she agreed, pointing out that there was plenty more where that came from.

"Any time," she said. "Any time."

And then they fell into silence as their bodies rode each other with that earnest dedication that only the extremely passionate or the starving can know.

After another rest she said, "Which one did you like the best? Which was the best time?"

"I dunno," Slocum said. "I'd have to try each one over again so I could make an honest comparison."

She burst out laughing. "What a great idea! Slocum, you are a genius! A very great man!" And as she grabbed his erection in her fist and looked down at it, she said, "I can't believe you're ready for more!"

"Aren't you?"

She didn't answer because she was already down on him, his great organ deep in her mouth, and she knew if she would have tried to speak she would gag.

Shortly, when she came up for air, he said, "My God, don't stop now."

"I'm not stopping, for God's sake; I'm simply catching my breath."

"Good enough," Slocum said. "Pardon the worry."

"I'll pardon anything, my dear, so long as I've got that delicious cock in my mouth."

But he barely heard her, for she was already proving her point, with his member deep in her mouth, down her throat, as she sucked and licked and fondled and drank him into their unbelievable union.

"Course, we kin start roundup early," Sonny Kitchen was saying. "That's what Nate did."

"That was the war then," his brother Jake pointed out, "and we all know what happened to poor Nate."

"That is for sure," put in Dusty Kitchen, as he stood in the middle of the corral with his two brothers. They were resting a moment after sacking a tough little mustang, who didn't like the sack, didn't like the rope, didn't like all the noise and action and clapping as he raced around the round corral—no corners to hide in—and looked wild-eyed and high-tailed enough to like maybe tear those three men apart.

They had run him and a few others in from up on the big tableland, and had cut out three for riding stuff, turning the rest loose. It was hard work and the Kitchen boys liked it. But their minds were really on something else.

"That is sure for sure," Dusty repeated. Exceptin' poor Nate got it; even though by God he did hold off a goddam army of them detectives and regulators with their shotguns, rifles, sidearms, burning haywagon and God knows all what else; till they got him. I heard they was forty-five of the sonofabitches at that shoot-out."

"Jesus," murmured Sonny. "They by God don't make 'em like that no more." His voice was stirred beyond mere admiration.

"Dunno about that," said Jake.

"Not countin' those present," Sonny said quickly, with a wink at brother Dusty.

Dusty said, "Puts me in mind of that feller Slocum, he does."

"Nate?"

Dusty nodded, spat reflectively at a pile of fresh horse manure, and reached to his shirt pocket for his makings.

"He is a tough boy," Jake said. "Can't say I'd see anybody backwaterin' him." And he canted his head at brother Dusty.

"Then whyn't we get him to help us?" Sonny said, his voice rising slightly as the exciting idea caught him.

"We already bin through that," Dusty Kitchen said. "And the answer is no."

"Whyn't we ask him agin?" Sonny insisted. "We need all the help that's about."

"Slocum is a man what keeps his nose clean, I've no doubt," Dusty Kitchen said. Then he lifted his forehead, pursed his mouth around the cigarette he'd just built and wet it, and squinted at his two younger brothers. "Could be we could ask him—nice like." Then he reached to his shirt pocket again and took out a wooden lucifer. He struck it one-handed on his thumbnail, bent his head to the flames, and squinted again at his brothers. "Where d'you reckon we'd find him?"

"He said he was headin' for Landusky," Jake said.

"I don't like leavin' the women," Dusty said. "I

got a real feeling that McGann is getting set for somethin'. You know why?''

"Same reason I figgered it," Jake said. "Don't see so many of his men about."

"Well, who's going in then? It'll have to be one of us." Dusty suddenly scratched his crotch. "Must be gettin' near Saturday," he said. And the three of them laughed at that, loosening themselves. "Goddam ticks bite harder than the fleas." He was looking at the youngest of the three, brother Sonny.

Sonny had been looking down at the ground, then moved his eyes to a block of salt in the corral that was pretty much hollowed out from the horses licking it. "All right then," he said. "I'll go."

"Try the saloons, the hotel, the cribs. And first of all the livery. Remember, he was riding that little Appaloosa."

"And what do I offer him?"

Dusty Kitchen shrugged. "What the hell can you offer him? We ain't got a pot to piss in out here. Just ask him. But don't hang around. Get yer ass back out here pronto!"

Sonny was already starting toward his saddle horse.

"And watch yer backtrail," Jake said. "And you got yer Winchester."

"Jesus," snapped Sonny, his eyes rolling about, as he stopped in his tracks and turned to face his two older brothers. "With you two old ladies, a man don't need a mother."

And though he was obviously bitter in his words, it was still good for them. All three saw that. It was good to be able still to complain and it was good too to see that Sonny was maybe growing up a piece.

• • •

When the boys in the saloon heard the train whistle in the distance they tossed down their drinks and went fast down to the depot. The big engine came pounding around the bend, its oil lamp, large as a bushel basket, gleaming into the early night, silhouetting the crowd standing on the station platform. It was one of the big events in Fiddler's Wells to go down and watch the Limited pull in, load up, and pull out on its way west.

Sparks from the big funnel were falling all over the depot, on top of the crowd watching, and also on the dry chips in the nearby lumberyards. On board, the brakemen spun the wheels that tightened the chains on the small brake shoes; and as the brakes took hold, the train staggered into a powerful halt. Almost as bad as any of the stagecoaches ever did, someone was sure to remark each time they witnessed it.

Collie, Heavy Bill Hames, Smitty, Duke, and Shadow Boy watched quietly from the black shadows of a pile of mine timbers. The night was still. Each of the five was heavily armed. They were wondering where the Kid was, for when he'd issued his orders back in the box canyon, he'd said that he would join them at the "right moment." Not that they believed him, but they knew he would catch up with them at some time or other, probably when they were least expecting him. It was the Kid's way to keep them guessing.

The Kid had given his orders carefully. The train would refuel at Hopp Corners, and also take on water. Therefore, the stop at Fiddler's Wells would be brief. They saw a brakeman wave a lantern; the engine belched a sizable amount from its firebox out of its funnel, sweeping the lumberyard, plus a good bit of area around it; and the train started with a tremendous jerk.

Collie and the boys didn't linger to see whether or not any fires were started by the shower of sparks. As the express car rolled past them, they grabbed the handgrips on the first passenger car and swung up onto its steps. As they came aboard, a brakeman was just starting to enter the coach.

A gasp broke from him when he realized he had company, and he made a grab for the door catch. Heavy Bill had a hold on him in an instant and rushed him across the car platform, and for a moment it looked as though they were both going to ditch the train, but it was only the brakeman who was unloaded. He landed in a pile of chips along the side of the tracks. And was instantly forgotten.

Shadow Boy and Duke at once began climbing to the top of the express car, Smitty and Collie supporting them over the swaying, jumping gap between the two cars. At this delicate moment the conductor just happened to appear, opening the door to see what had delayed the brakeman.

"Shut the door," Heavy Bill said. "You're making a draft."

The conductor swiftly realized the backup in those simple—if polite—words as he saw the massive armaments accompanying those non-paying passengers, and he shut the door without further discussion.

Collie and Heavy Bill now made their way over the top of the express car to the tender, which was stacked high with chunks of wood for the firebox. It was no simple exercise climbing over these. Then, just as they clambered over the top of the pile, the fireman opened the firebox and turned toward the pile to throw in more wood. The two outlaws could be seen clearly in the glaring yellow and orange of the shooting flames.

And at that instant the front of the pile of wood gave way and Collie and Heavy Bill slid right down into the cab. The fireman's shout of surprise and alarm coupled with the avalanche of wood dropping down into the cab frightened the engineer into a moment of paralysis. This afforded Heavy Bill and Collie enough time to draw their weapons, though Heavy Bill was half buried in the pile of wood, and not all that mobile. It was Collie who took over control of the locomotive.

About a mile north of Hopp Corners, at a convenient level stretch of track, Collie ordered the engineer to stop the train. As he did so, Smitty, at the other end of the train, received the signal and immediately set the brake on the passenger cars and pulled out the coupling pin that linked them to the express car. This task was executed neatly and he called out to Collie that the job was done.

Collie nodded toward the throttle bar as the frozen engineer looked at him. But the man refused to move.

"Shit!" snapped Collie, but he was not without resources. Stepping swiftly forward he shoved the engineer aside and took over. But though he had no difficulty in getting the engine to move, a short way ahead they entered a long, twisting downgrade and immediately the engine began to pick up speed. Swiftly, Collie closed the throttle, but by that time they were already hurtling down, their speed accelerated by the steep drop.

Collie looked about desperately for the brakes, but his engineering experience was severely limited and the instruments in the big cab defied him. But help came through the character of the older engineer. Evidently, he was quite satisfied, indeed happy, to defy the bandits who had taken over his train, but it was quite another thing to risk losing his beloved engine.

Seeing his situation, plus the sure knowledge that they'd probably all get killed including himself, he suddenly pushed Collie aside and grabbed the brake, pulling back on it just as the big train hurtled into a sharp bend. Luck was with them, for the man at the brakes applied them with professional instinct and experience. Slowly the big pounding train came under control.

Shoving his gun barrel into the engineer's back, Collie ordered him to stay where he was or he'd be "deader'n a doornail quicker'n a rabbit can lick his own balls."

Then he was running back to the express car. His fellow bandits were already there. Shadow Boy was pounding on the door of the car.

"Who is it? What's the matter?" the express clerk called through the closed door. Clearly the wild movement of the train and the unscheduled stop had warned him of trouble.

Collie didn't waste even a precious second in shooting out the lock of the door. When he pushed the door back and burst in, the terrified expressman was standing with lifted arms at the side of the car, offering not the least resistance. At the same time Heavy Bill and Shadow Boy swarmed into the express car with Collie; the remaining two, Duke and Smitty, stayed outside, alert to any unexpected moves from the passengers or remaining crew.

Inside the express car Collie, Heavy Bill, and Shadow Boy covered the shaking expressman. Seeing he was alone, Collie ordered Shadow Boy to join the two outside who were standing guard.

The interior of the dingy car was illuminated by a brace of coal oil lamps suspended from the ceiling. At the front end was the mail compartment, separated from the express compartment by a wooden partition. There was a closed door in the center of the partition, and the mail clerk could be heard moving about on the inside.

"Mail?" Heavy Bill cocked an eyebrow at Collie. He would have been happy to batter down the flimsy door, or even the whole partition, with his huge fists.

Collie shook his head. "Who can read, for Chrissakes?"

The express box containing the gold they sought stood in the center of the car. There was a fire axe on the wall, and Collie seized it and with one stroke split the wooden box wide open. A shower of gold coins flew out of the demolished box, a number of which rolled in various directions over the floor. All the other boxes in the car were treated to the same attack, providing they showed the possibility of inner wealth. Heavy Bill was already filling the sacks they had brought along for that purpose. Collie went to the door and called out for someone to come and help.

They worked quickly passing down the gold, and when they were done they leaped out of the car. Collie signaled the engineer to back out onto the main line and hook up with the rest of the train. The train moved out slowly.

The men found their horses where they'd tied them to be at the ready, and loaded them with their wealth. The horses snorted and two reared.

"Jesus," said Collie to nobody in particular. "I hope that sonofabitch don't take a notion to pull his whistle."

"We'll all be gone to hell over half of Wyoming and Texas if he do," said Heavy Bill.

But providence, or something, was with the boys this night, and the engineer did not pull his whistle.

They waited until the locomotive had backed around the first bend and was out of sight.

It was a brilliant night with a full moon as the five highly successful bandits rode toward the rendezvous in the box canyon country; yet each knowing that in truth he was riding toward the Kid. And each in his own way was wondering where the Kid was. And what he would say when he saw what a good job they'd pulled.

They hadn't gone very far when they found out. Simultaneously the five heard the horse gaining on them. Swiftly they spread out, guns drawn, ready to shoot whoever it might be right out of the saddle.

But something must have interfered with the rider's destiny, for suddenly they heard the hooves fade away, as though he'd veered off the trail.

They were standing beside their mounts, trying to decide whether to push on, or to get some rest and travel by daylight, when suddenly they heard the familiar voice, slipping easily into the brisk night air.

"You boys lookin' for me, was you? Figurin' you'd gun me when I come ridin' up?"

And there he was, standing right in the middle of the trail ahead of them, his loose grin taking over all the slackness of his pale face. And with that terrible cut-down twelve-gauge in his hands.

"I got a packhorse with me, boys," the Kid said, grinning at them. "You boys can load him up. Then you can head for the canyon. I'll see you there in a day or two." And he suddenly let go his frightening, whinnying laugh; the sound of which was always more terrifying to the five than his out-and-out anger.

Under the prodding eyes of the Kid it didn't take long to transfer the gold to the handy panniers on his pack animal. And it was all done in silence.

They watched the Kid ride off. Nothing was said. At any rate, not until they were sure he was well out of earshot.

It was the volatile Smitty who broke the severe silence in which they had been wrapped.

"By God, lookee at this here! Where is our share! That feller, he is the most dishonest man I have ever seen in the whole of my entire life!"

7

At Crazy Woman Basin business was booming. Landusky had already set up a lively pop-skull palace, with whiskey, beer, cards, and dice; all the niceties and necessities for cowboy, cattleman, or drifter to relax and spend his money the happy way. He had just now decided to bring one-legged Luther Bones down to run the operation, for he expected an influx of even more business just as soon as Lily got her establishment going, and he wanted a good man running things, someone who knew the business forwards and back and could and would keep his mouth shut. Luther, with his shotgun-crutch, was just the man for the action. And anyway, his previous manager had expired in a passage at arms over a misunderstanding at cards. Just as well; Luther was perfect for the job.

And Miles Landusky just knew he would be proven right. Luther would run the business with an iron hand, and—more important—with profit and with total fealty to his employer.

And in the meanwhile, the depredations of the "outlaw element," as the newpaper editorials in the *Rocky Mountain Declaimer* called them, had increased. In response to this great surge of highway robbery, murder, arson, and general terrorizing of the populace, Miles Landusky had raised his voice, his editorial sword—the pen!—and declaimed loud and clear that "something has to be done!" The tireless yet always useful strategy of the crook supposedly chasing the crook.

Landusky knew that his projection regarding the establishment of Lily and her business in Crazy Woman Basin could only reap high profit, not only for his saloon but for his further enterprise under the able hand of Use Moriarty, operating out of the box canyons up near Betty Creek. His only worry, as he now confided to Lily while they sat together sipping whiskey, was that she might work herself to death.

"But I save it for you, honey. You gotta know that!" she said, snuggling against his big chest. She loved it when he teased her that way.

"Just remember that," Landusky said blandly, for he was already thinking of something else. But then catching the look of mild surprise on her face at his lack of attention, he said quickly, "You know how I favor your charms, young lady. Yours—uh—exclusively." And he immediately wondered if she was thinking that, of course, with that face, how could he do otherwise?

But Lily wasn't even thinking of his face, as she reached over and began stroking his knee. Lily had learned that there was only one way to handle a man, and that was to handle him. Indeed, this sage rule, which she'd known instinctively most of her life, had been formulated verbally for her by Landusky himself shortly after their first carnal encounter.

"I expect business to be as big as you can handle," he was now saying to her as he refilled their glasses, and her hand rose along his thigh. "But I don't want you to overdo it."

"Am I handling this all right?" she said, squeezing his growing organ.

They both chuckled at that.

"I've something special I want to talk to you about," he said, his voice suddenly serious.

"I'm listening."

"You're not listening," he said. "You're only thinking of getting screwed. Now cut it out!"

And suddenly he was hard. Suddenly he was whip-cord and steel. She had only seen him like that once before, when he'd blasted that one-legged saloonkeeper into line over something or other. And at the time she'd been terrified. She was right now. Her breath stopped, she had to control her knees from shaking.

Yet at the same time she knew she was sitting still, with no giveaway in her face. She had her courage. Hell, didn't you have to have it, with her kind of job!

The thought braced her as, without removing her hand, she put herself totally on guard, her insides closed.

"Remember," he said, "that you and Bones are the only ones here who know I've got this place." He grinned suddenly, feeling his face move into the posture of grinning; and he wondered for a split second how she saw him. He knew what he looked like, for he'd spent considerable time making various facial expressions in front of a mirror so that he would know. And it gave him a certain satisfaction to note the reactions of various people when he revealed himself in this way. But the girl didn't react. Perhaps he'd jolted her pretty strongly just now. Good then. Keep 'em in line; one way or another, though mostly, by God, one way.

"I already forgot about it," she said.

"That's the girl," he said, and he covered her hand with his.

He saw that she was waiting for him to tell her what he had started to say. He let her wait. And he was pleased in a strange way to see that she had control of herself. She'd been rattled for a moment when he'd snapped at her, but now she had herself back in one piece. Of course, he could have taken her apart. And he just might, though only when the need appeared. Never waste your ammo, was the idea. You never know when you might need it for something more important.

Her hand was firm on his erection now, stroking it through his trousers. And he could feel his breath catching, speeding up, catching again as he got harder. Christ, what was it about her that got him so goddam hot!

Suddenly he sat up. Christ again, how many top men had been hit when they had their pants down! By damn, not him! He wasn't going to let his cock do his thinking for him. Business first, by God, and watch your backtrail!

She had drawn back, her face coloring just slightly, so slightly that only his eagle eye perceived it. Good. You had to keep them off balance in order to rule.

"I got something special I want you to do," he said. He sniffed, his erection softening. "Like I was saying."

"Just tell me what it is, hon."

"You'll be seeing a lot of people. Men. At your place."

"Well, I hope so. Ain't that the notion?"

He grinned at her, with the tip of his tongue between his teeth. She was smart, all right. Of course she had to be to keep up with himself.

Still he waited, watching her. She had guts, and he liked that. You didn't meet a lot of whores like that. Tough, sure. Sharp, seductive, they were all that. But this one—and for a flash he wondered if her name was really Lily—this one was something else. Somehow—he didn't know how to say it, how to tell it to himself—somehow she had something different, something—private, was the word that came. Something of her own? It was beyond him; and for an instant he felt the well-known jealousy. But strangely it passed, and he didn't mind anymore. Hell, was he getting old, crazy? Too long in the tooth to demand his existence, his life, any longer? But he shoved the thought aside; and yet, even then, he remembered "Old" Ted Zachary who had tried to teach him back in Massachusetts, back at Cambridge. Shit, he hadn't cracked a book since; yet he remembered "Old Zack," drooling over some goddam poet or some such. And he was suddenly speaking to her.

"I want you to tell me who comes there. Who you see."

"Anyone special?" The question was gentle; even so he could feel her curiosity. Well, it might spur her to look harder.

"Just notice like if somebody is different. See? Maybe the way he carries his hardware. Maybe he looks young, but he's old; or maybe the other way round. Things like that. Anyone that doesn't look regular, ordinary."

"Got it," she said.

They fell silent then, and at length she said, "I could tell you about someone I already met."

"Yeah? Who?"

She felt a little bounce of pleasure, yet mixed with some fear too, as he bit at the bait. But she too sometimes liked risk.

"A nice feller," she said with a slow smile, reaching forward and squeezing his erection. "A real friendly feller, and he's gotten to be a habit with me."

And then he was laughing. They were both laughing. He jumped to his feet and lifted her, chair and all, and bore her swiftly to the unmade bed.

In seconds they were naked and she was down on him, taking him all the way into her mouth, down her throat.

After they had done it three times, in her mouth, between her legs front, and from behind, she said, "Thought you was concerned about me overdoing things."

"I was," he said.

"What about now?"

"Jesus Christ," he said, pretending a frown. "Don't you know with all your experience that the only time a man's sensible and can be trusted is after he's had it?"

She smiled patiently at him then. "Hon, that's just why I always have my customers pay in advance. Didn't you know that?"

He had tried his hand at the faro table, sat in for a few hands at draw poker, and laid down some dollars on the ivories. After two, three hours Slocum had come out with about what he'd started with. Even the wheel of fortune, which he tried next, didn't turn up anything.

Prior to all that he'd stopped in at the barber, had a bath, a shave, listened to the country gossip, laid out some feelers; and—nothing. Landusky was a town that seemed quite satisfied to be just a town.

Yet something kept him here at the Elkhorn. He sure couldn't figure what. It wasn't the gaming. It wasn't the terrible whiskey, which somebody said if you didn't piss it out, it'd burn a hole through your bladder; and it wasn't the girls.

And so he remained. There was just no arguing with his feeling about the place. And he knew from long experience that the only way to find out what it was, was to find out what it was. No horsefeathers in that, no fancy-pants thinking; just good hoss sense.

The Elkhorn was a long, thin room with a low ceiling and a wooden plank bar that ran the entire length of the floor, with just enough room for the big bartender with the sloping, pear-shaped body to get in and out. His name was Cornelius, and he was chatty. Slocum engaged him in an endless conversation that as far as he was concerned got nowhere. It finally occurred to him that perhaps Cornelius had been hired for just that purpose: conversation that said nothing. The man was talented, Slocum had to admit. He could take more words to say absolutely nothing than anyone Slocum had ever met anywhere—man, woman, or child.

All the same, Cornelius was clearly well liked and even respected by his customers.

From time to time Slocum wandered over to watch one of the card or dice games, or even walked into the next room to watch the dancing. The orchestra offered threadbare renditions of such favorites as

"Chicken in the Breadtray" and "Old Dan Tucker"; everyone still careful not to play anything that savored of the blue or the gray; feelings being what they still were. Although not as severe as in some parts of the country.

Nor did the girls appeal to him. He kept thinking of Jillie McGann and realized that in that sense he'd been spoiled. She had spoiled him for any lesser fare, and the pickings at the Elkhorn bore testimony to this. Still, he enjoyed watching the dancers cavort about the floor. And so he remained, still with the feeling almost amounting to a certainty that something would sooner or later show up that would give him an opening into how the town felt about the Kitchens and their comrades, and the McGann bunch and theirs.

To be sure, having been well blooded in at least two big range controversies, he knew the signs. He could smell how the townfolk felt, knew instinctively who was likely to win out and what means would be called in—special regulators or range detectives, to use the fancied-up names—high explosives, guns, and of course top gunmen. He already knew that the little men didn't have a chance. Nevertheless, he had caught the smell of something more than a mere range war.

To begin with, the graze where the Kitchens were located wasn't all that good, nor was the water so accessible. It was the same with their neighbors. Studying the location of the McGann outfit and those others that were linked with it revealed the fact that the big stockmen already had everything they needed—good graze and access to the mountain for summer grazing, and plenty of water at whatever location they'd find desirable. In fact, the big men weren't hurting at all, and it had looked to him that they were provoking the smaller men for some other purpose. Or, as the Kitchens had said, the big men were angried up because they claimed their beeves were being rustled and rebranded with running irons.

To be sure, this was a not uncommon practice on the open range. Many small outfits got their start by roping out slicks from someone else's herd before roundup time and slapping a brand on them. And until recently that practice had been mildly acceptable. A calf or so here, another there. But when it came to reworking an outfit's brand on grown beef cattle, that was a step further than tolerance could accept.

Yet the Kitchens had vowed to Slocum that they had never—except for a slick here or there, and some time in the past—never dropped their iron on Mc-Gann's or anyone else's stock. And Slocum believed them. Indeed, as he'd told them, a man would be a damn fool, looking for a hole in his head or his guts or a rope around his neck, to try such a dumb thing on a man such as Tom McGann and his likes.

And there the trail ended. He could think it through that far, see the arguments on each side; but it didn't add up. The way the valley was set up nobody in his right mind would try pulling anything like cutting in on a big herd.

Slocum stood at the bar again, taking his drink slowly, his eyes on the crowded tables, watching the ease with which the hefty Cornelius moved. His big belly kept pushing the planking out of line as he moved up and down the bar, and every once in a while he'd have to stop to adjust the rig so the whole thing wouldn't collapse.

Slocum had noticed that the game of poker at the table in the little alcove at the far end of the room had been going on for as long as he'd been in the place, and had likely started well before he'd arrived. The boys had looked to be really into the action when he'd paused to watch a short while before.

Now, feeling again that something might happen, hoping that it would happen, and indeed with that special sense in himself knowing that something was in fact going to happen, he drifted over to the little alcove with his drink.

He saw right away that it was the same high-stakes game of poker. He had figured out the players by now, had heard their names, and even caught snatches of conversation from other watchers as to who they were.

There was a drummer named Harvey; a cattle dealer, Fred Standish; and two professional gamblers named Sauk Thoms and Bigjaw Pete Thrush.

The game had been going smoothly for a good while, with now and again some of the clientele coming over to see how things were going. The boys were drinking, though by no means heavily. The action was decidedly friendly. And the stakes were within reasonable limits. Nothing big or dramatic. But Slocum noticed that by now, Cornelius, the huge bartender, had turned his office behind the planks over to someone else and had come to oversee the game. Slocum remembered that he had noticed Cornelius throwing glances over toward the alcove every so often. He obviously was feeling some kind of concern. And by now Slocum had figured him for the manager or possibly even owner of the place. At any rate, the big man had arrived and stood solid as a small mountain just between and in back of Sauk Thoms and Bigjaw Pete Thrush, his eyes sharp as a bird's as they pecked back and forth over the play.

At last a hand brought real money to the table, and

the pot grew until the final call. At that point Bigjaw Pete laid down a hand with two aces and Sauk Thoms one with three. Swift as a wink Cornelius stepped in as self-appointed referee and, snatching up the fifth ace, ruled that all bets were off, that the pot should remain intact and a fresh hand he dealt. His wide, soft hands tore up the fifth ace into little pieces, revealing to Slocum that the man was stronger than he looked.

But a crowd had quickly gathered about the table, and as the players picked up their cards tension mounted. As someone later mentioned in the countless retellings, the tension was as thick as the cigar smoke.

Following the next draw, the raises and back raises hit swiftly until only Sauk Thoms and Bigjaw Pete Thrush were left in the game. This time when the two hands were laid down, Sauk Thoms laid down two aces, but Thrush spread three on the torn green baize.

This time for some reason unknown there was no intervening on the part of Cornelius who to Slocum's surprise had stepped back from the scene. With one hand, his right, Bigjaw Pete drew the pot toward him, and with his left he drew a gun and shot Thoms, who, covered with blood, slumped down under the table.

Bigjaw assumed that he had his pot then, but the other players made a grab for it, wanting their share. As they argued over the justice and/or injustice of the point, Thoms rose from beneath the table and shot Bigjaw Pete, killing him. This accomplished, he slid back down to the floor. Dead.

However, this did not settle the question of the pot. Now, before the other two players could carry things further, Cornelius ruled that they should have all that they'd bet. And before anybody could even get an argument together on this decision, Cornelius ruled that the rest of the money belonged to the house.

But this wasn't satisfactory, and so Cornelius turned to the gaping onlookers and on the spot impaneled a coroner's jury. "Landusky is and always has been a law-abidin' town," he deponed, looking directly at Slocum, for no reason that Slocum, an innocent onlooker, could fathom.

The impaneled jury acted swiftly, for Cornelius had offered the bait of free drinks to anyone supporting "the wheels of justice." Cornelius himself was clearly a bit the worse for wear now, as Slocum realized.

The jury returned a quick verdict that the two deaths had been due to "natural causes." In searching Thrush's clothing two aces were discovered in his belt. While a third was discovered in one of Thoms's pockets.

The room broke into a vigorous though not unruly uproar at that point, and a brisk argument followed as to how, when, and where the two card mechanics should be buried.

The orchestra in the next room now broke into a rendition of "Auld Lang Syne," house drinks were served to those who had served the cause of justice by volunteering for jury, while the rest of the clientele addressed themselves to further refreshment at their own expense.

John Slocum did the same. He had just turned his back to the room when he heard someone say his name. And to his surprise he saw that it was Sonny Kitchen, with a shy grin on his face, his blond hair falling into his eyes, which were bugging with excitement.

Suddenly the atmosphere, the very smell of the barroom, had changed. Slocum sensed it the moment he saw Sonny Kitchen in the mirror approaching him, heard him say his name, caught the twitch of alarm in Cornelius the big bartender's buried eyes. Cornelius's fat face had turned white, then a flush appeared, as evidently his anger came to his rescue.

They were three; two of them part of the trio that Slocum had braced out on the McGann range when he'd met Jillie McGann. The third man he'd not seen before. He watched them in the mirror, right after nodding to Sonny; saw them as he heard the thwack of the swinging door that they pushed open, as though cutting a hole in the side of the building.

There was still the music drifting in from the next room, the clink of chips could be heard, the clearing of throats and the wet whistle of streaking tobacco juice shooting from pursed lips and thonking into a spittoon or missing, as the case might be. Life went on. But it was sure different.

"Howdy," Slocum said without turning his head, but speaking to Sonny in the mirror. "Have one."

"Sure will." Sonny, his pale eyes large, luminous, and staring, tried not to look at the three McGann men who had now reached the bar, upon which Cornelius already had placed a bottle and three glasses. They had moved through the throng like a scythe parting a field of wheat. And as they reached for their drinks, it was as though the town—or at any rate the Elkhorn—lay before them.

They had obviously been drinking before their arrival. Slocum checked their armaments. Each had a gun at his hip, and each looked as though he knew well enough how to use that weapon. He was particularly watching the two who had been out on the range. The one he had backwatered was not present, but his two companions had clearly taken note of him. They were looking at him, sneering and talking to each other, obviously telling the third man who he was.

Cornelius was now standing before them, his eyelids heavy and halfway down over his great bronze eyeballs as he addressed Slocum and Sonny.

"It won't be considered out of line if you two men take a notion to leave these premises," the fat bartender said, speaking softly, and mostly from the side of his mouth, while his eyes, hardly visible now behind his puffy cheeks, observed them carefully for reaction. "Course, that be up to you," he added.

"We'll be having another round," Slocum said.

Cornelius nodded, almost imperceptibly. "Figured so," he muttered. "Turnin' out to be quite a evenin', ain't it—with them two ace magicians and now this here."

Wagging his head slowly from side to side, he ambled down the length of the bar, lifted a bottle from in front of an old-timer who looked as though he was about to collapse, and returned with it to Slocum and his companion.

"Though I got to say I would 'preciate you two takin' a walk," he said. "Some of this furniture is brand new and thing is it always breaks easy." He nodded his pointed head backwards. "Couple times ago they busted that whole mirror piece. You can guess who had to pay for it."

"If there's any trouble," Slocum said, "it won't be us starting it."

The big man's face lengthened even more; he looked fit for a funeral. "That's what I know, mister. But I figger you for the kind who'll finish it; if necessary over everybody else's body." He leaned his hands on the bar now, his arms straight out, his narrow shoulders hunched, the rest of him sagging like a huge pile of damp laundry. "Just trying to keep the peace, sir."

"Maybe tell them that," Slocum suggested, "since you've already figured they'll start it."

"Just remember there is two of us," Sonny said to Slocum. "You won't be alone."

At this, the magisterial figure on the other side of the bar looked down his sloping torso as though at something indistinct, and said, "Son, if you want to be able to ride your horse back home to the Hardwater you'd be smart to take my advice. I know this friend of yours here ain't even listening."

Slocum watched Sonny's cheeks color, but the boy held his tongue. Slocum reached for the bottle.

Suddenly a shout came down the length of the bar. "Hey, bring that bottle back here." It was one of the three, who had moved up to stand beside the old-timer who had been the last to pour from it.

"Send the boy down with it, and don't take all day!"

"Take it slow," Slocum said fast, keeping his voice down so that only Sonny heard it. He could tell how nervous the boy was, but he also saw how he was handling it. Yes, for sure he was like those two brothers. Softer, but not soft. He could see how that would fool a lot of people. And indeed it was obviously fooling the man who had shouted for the bottle.

"Sonny boy. Bring that bottle like a good little kid, will ya?"

The room had stopped. There was only the sound of a single poker chip falling into a pile of its companions with a click that in any other circumstances would have passed unnoticed, but now sounded pretty damn loud.

"Don't move," Slocum said softly to the boy.

"Hey there, kid, I said bring the bottle. Or do you got to ask permission from that busted-down bronc chaser. Huh? Daddy got yer tongue, kid?"

Slocum had been taking in every detail of the three men. There was definitely something missing, but for the moment he didn't know what.

"C'mon, Red, let's haul outta this place. It stinks of shit here." This suggestion was voiced by one of the companions of the man who had spoken.

"Sonny boy don't want to play," said the third man, the one who had not been with the others out on the prairie where Slocum had met the other two.

But Red was reddening now in his big flat face. He spat furiously in the direction of a cuspidor, getting something on the boot of one of his companions, but still with his eyes on Slocum and Sonny.

"Hey you, mister. Wanna let the little boy bring along that bottle?" And he threw back his head and laughed. And started to move down the bar toward Slocum and Sonny. But he had obviously drunk a great deal and he was staggering, almost falling down, as his two companions spread out, with their hands close to their six-guns.

Red was close now, and Slocum could smell the whiskey on him. It almost smelled like too much. He had rarely smelled the booze so strongly on another man like that. Red was almost on top of them now, his hands sewing the air in front of him, staggering as though not only drunk but blind.

And then Slocum got it. Of course that was what was missing.

"Dive!" he snapped at Sonny, as he dropped to one knee, drawing his Colt in a single lightning motion and firing at the figure that was standing just inside the batwing doors of the saloon.

His shot was true, hitting the man whom he had beaten when he'd spat at him out on the trail. In no longer than the next breath he covered them all—the two who now stood frozen at the bar, plus the one who was standing in front of him.

"Slick little trick, but you dumb shits gave it away," he said, his tone cold as ice. "Drop those gunbelts. And you . . ." He pointed his gun at the man who had been coming toward them as a distraction for the bushwhacker at the door. "You—come here."

The man took a step forward.

"Closer!"

"Listen, Slocum, I didn't mean no harm!"

"But, mister, I do!" And in a flash he had slammed the man in the belly with the barrel of his six-gun, stepped back giving him room to double over, then with his left fist smashed him behind the ear. The apologetic victim delivered himself to the hard floor of the Elkhorn, accompanied by the astonished gasps and gaping mouths of the onlookers.

Slocum still had the other two right under his Colt .36.

"Strip!"

He didn't have to repeat it. Both gunbelts thumped to the floor.

"I said *strip!*"

The pair froze, their mouths hanging open like a pair of wagon endgates.

"Right now!" And a bullet hit the floor inches from their feet. In a minute they were down to their long-handles.

Another bullet hit just at their feet.

"Strip! You sonsofbitches. I mean right down. All of it!"

In less than a minute the pair were naked. They

stood there barefooted and—as an old miner muttered, not too loudly; but he was observant, somebody later noted sardonically—bare-assed.

"Now git. Take them two with you."

"He ain't dead," someone said, speaking from the swinging doors. "Hit the man plumb center in his gun hand. I take that to be intentional!" the speaker added loudly, covering himself with awe at the scene they had all just beheld.

"Jesus . . ." The single word cut the silence that had fallen into the frozen barroom. It was uttered by Cornelius from behind the wooden planking of his bar. He stood there like an astonished Solomon as the naked pair limped out with their two companions following.

The awesome exclamation clearly bore repeating as someone else said the second word to enter the great silence.

"Christ . . ."

This word was uttered by the marshal of Landusky, Luther Bones, who now arrived on the scene, limping with the aid of his shotgun-crutch, cursing at each step at the pain of it, or the aggravation, or with simple old-fashioned impatience at being hampered by fate, bullets, or both.

"Who done it?" the marshal demanded.

"I did. And it was self-defense." Slocum said the words clear and loud.

"We'll see about that. Man shooting up four of Tom McGann's men, well, you kin figger to be in some kind of trouble, mister."

"I shot one man," Slocum said, "who was trying to dry-gulch me, set up by the other three."

"That's the truth," cut in Sonny Kitchen.

"You with him, Kitchen? I think that says it all."

Marshal Bones motioned with his six-gun. "Unbuckle that gun of yourn and march. The both of yez!" And he brandished the six-gun again. "You're both under arrest."

The silence that followed those words resounded through Slocum's body like a military drumroll.

The jail was a log cabin directly in back of the marshal's office, the frame building that was at the same time saloon, clothing store, and living quarters. The latter included Mrs. Bones, a bedraggled harpy with a front tooth missing, a leer as she regarded the two prisoners, and a tongue that surely had been dipped in vinegar.

"About time you wuz startin' to earn somethin' for playin' law an' order around this town. Damn jail was about to fall down from rot 'fore you ever latched onto a bona fide prisoner." Her orange eyes took in Slocum and Sonny Kitchen. "Least you caught yerself a pair what looks halfway decent," she said, throwing a lecherous look that made Slocum's heart lose a couple of beats.

"There are fates worse than death," he said, turning toward his young companion. "Brace yourself, young feller."

But Sonny had no time to answer, for they were entering the cabin.

"Circuit rider'll be along sometime this month," the marshal said. "You two make yerselves to home." And with an angry sniff in their direction he closed the door of the cabin.

They listened to the key being turned in the padlock outside.

"Sometime this month!" Sonny's voice was filled with the deepest dismay. "We can't stay here that long. There is all that work to be done out at the outfit.''

"It looks like it might have to be done without us,'' Slocum said. ''Those logs look pretty well set,'' he went on, as he walked over to examine them more closely.

"Slocum, what are we going to do?"

"Wait."

"Wait! Wait for what? The circuit rider?"

"I don't think so." Slocum had sat down on the pile of bedding that lay rolled up in one corner of the cabin. He was busy inspecting their quarters.

"Dirt floor,'' he said. ''We could start digging." He stood up and walked over and put his hand on the log wall.

"Yeah!" Sonny's face brightened.

"Except someone'd be waiting for us when we got to the outside and we'd have just wasted all of ourselves on doing something dumb.''

"But what else can we do?"

Slocum had studied the walls while he spoke to Sonny, and now he stood in the middle of the dirt floor studying the roof. It was made of rough lumber, but he could see it was strongly nailed, and maybe even screwed to the walls.

"We'd never get through there without somebody catching on to us,'' he said. ''What about the door? I looked at it pretty close when we came in. But . . .'' And he strode to the thick lumber door, with new hardware holding it firmly and—as far as he could tell—unassailably in place.

He stood there, watching his companion, shaking his head slowly. ''Not much chance there, my friend.''

"So what can we do?" Sonny's voice rose, and Slocum easily caught the worry in it.

"Nothing," he said.

"Shit."

"Yup." He sighed and sat down cross-legged on some of the bedding.

"But we could wait here forever," Sonny almost wailed.

"I've got a notion it won't be too long," Slocum said, taking out the makings and starting to build a smoke.

"How you figger that? It looks to me like we're in here forever and then might likely get a necktie party."

"I don't think so." Slocum struck the wooden lucifer along the bottom of his thigh and bent his head to the flame. Speaking around the cigarette he was holding in his lips, he said, "I don't reckon we'll have too long to wait till Mr. Tom McGann shows up."

8

Big Tom McGann sat in his big chair in his big office in the middle of his big ranch and watched the drop of water that was hanging on the end of his visitor's thin, pale, long nose. He wondered if the man knew it was there. He supposed he should, for, hell, the man had a rep for speed, reflex, accuracy, and it was said he could count the seconds watching a man die.

"I think that ought to give you a picture of the way of it hereabouts," he said, having just summed up the situation in the feud involving the stockgrowers and the small cattlegrowers.

His visitor nodded. He had not removed his hat, though in that country there was nothing unusual about that. The hat was basic to a cowboy, and even some gunmen. It was said that when a cow waddie got up in the morning the first thing he did was put on his hat.

It looked to Tom McGann that the man slouching

in the chair across from him never took his off. Ever. Same with that sidearm. He'd been hearing for a long time about the speed and accuracy of that weapon; and especially the man behind it. It was, he'd been told, a Russian model Smith & Wesson .44, specially designed for the czar's army, with a butt much slimmer and more sharply curved than the Frontier model. Interesting point, the fact that the man took it as important to have something special like that. What was it, for instance, in that silly-looking overgrown kid that would make him pick something out of the ordinary for his weapon? He knew; actually he knew, but he couldn't necessarily put it into words. He knew some killers were like that; had to fancy things up. Funny. Why couldn't a man be just what he was? Like himself. Plain, honest man, hardworking, always dealing it straight.

The feller there looked like a snake, with those thick pale eyelids that dropped over those pink-rimmed, watery eyes that by God never seemed to blink.

"You'll be wanting me to bring men," the Kid said.

"Bring what you've got. I can always use extra. What I am saying is have them handy. Yerself, I don't want you to show much. I am running my business here aboveboard. You understand."

"I do." The two words fell into the conversation like two chips of ice.

McGann felt himself getting angry, but instantly let it go. He was about to say something to modify his position, but refused the luxury; yes, he realized the sudden weakness to justify. But he was a man who was accustomed to taking the initiative, and so he stood up.

To his surprise his visitor remained seated.

"The money."

McGann felt the color coming into his face.

"I get paid in advance."

"I was not told that."

"I'm telling you now."

But McGann had control of himself now. He hadn't built an empire by backing down, but also he hadn't built what he had out there and right here by being stupid.

He said, "Go take a walk around. Have a look at things. I'll have the money time you get back, twenty minutes. It'll be what we agreed on for two weeks; then we'll see where we are."

The Kid was on his feet now, the sneer still on his face. It crossed the rancher's mind that maybe it had always been there; well, at any rate as long as he'd been what he was now. But the thought was fleeting, hardly acknowledged.

"I'll send for you in about fifteen, twenty minutes," he said at the door. And as he said that he felt the pull of pleasure at having regained himself, at having euchred the Kid. Indeed, he had the money in his desk, had known all along that the Kid always demanded payment in advance. But he knew too that he, Tom McGann, had to be in control; that he was in control. And no monkey business about that.

But he was totally unprepared for what happened then. He had spoken to the Kid's back as he went ahead of him through the door. In the hallway outside, his visitor turned. He looked even more pale and scaly than he had sitting in the armchair while they'd discussed his duties. And standing there, he appeared to have on even more clothing than before, almost as though he were lost inside the big trail coat, the grimy red bandanna around his neck, and with the pale, fishy white of his slender hands that protruded from the scruffy cuffs. The rancher had already noted how the nails on both hands were chewed right down; it seemed almost to the quick.

At just that moment the outside door opened and Jillie walked into the hallway. McGann felt her presence hit him like a blow in the guts. A blow of pleasure at the very sight of her, the apple of his eye, yet at the same time a gong of alarm ran through him all the way and he felt something leaving him at the same time. It was a sensation he had never before experienced; and it shook him. But once more he regained himself, exchanged a family glance with her as she passed swiftly by. He knew his visitor must have seen her out of the side of his eye, and it was then that McGann especially felt the fear. And with the Kid's parting words suffused his body; words so totally unlike the person uttering them, so foreign to that deadly person that he felt himself turn cold.

"Thank you, Mr. McGann."

In the light of the coal oil lamp the editor and publisher of the *Rocky Mountain Declaimer* sat busily at his crowded desk. He wrote quickly, with strong, stern strokes of his pen. As always Miles Landusky was enjoying his work; sometimes frowning, sometimes chuckling at what appeared on the sheet of paper before him.

"It is only a question of whether an editor dies by whiskey or gunpowder," he wrote. "The powder, generally being of better quality than the whiskey, usually accomplishes its end first."

He sat back chuckling. It would liven the page. Sure, he'd cribbed it. But then editors were always stealing from one another, just like the stockgrowers, and everyone else.

Now, picking up a copy of a rival paper he read, "We want a story every morning that will justify someone's waking us up before noon with a gun and the promise of sudden death."

For sure, he was thinking. And if the job of staying alive wasn't enough, there were more than a few other problems. For one item, the lack of paper. He personally, in his short career as editor, had resorted a number of times to putting out the whole edition on brown wrapping paper. And too, there had been the problem of distribution. He had also delivered his papers on horseback as far away as fifty miles, until he'd made enough to hire a boy for the job. Ah, it hadn't been easy.

Funny, he'd wanted to be an editor back home, back at school and college. And by damn he'd come west with that aim in mind, but then . . . Then, what had happened? He wasn't sure. He did know that there was a link between his wish for the world of the newspaper and what had finally happened to him.

He'd been taken on in Virginia City, a young man, a kid really, but he'd been glad to be an all-round "boy" for the *Enterprise*. He'd learned a lot. And then he'd met Ives Banning, who offered him a job as a copier on his *Montana Times*. The next thing he knew he was involved in work on the paper up to his neck every day in the week, and nights too until the deadline was met. And then Ives had introduced him to his second work, his sideline of robbing stagecoaches; an enterprise at which his employer excelled until one day he was cut in two by three shotgun messengers firing at once.

It was then that the young man who had changed

his name to Butch Killigan came into his own. From then on he had followed his twin career with full vigor. And he had discovered the germs for his present enterprise in Landusky. He had discovered that there was great interest—and money—in fighting what he had then spoken of editorially as "the ruthless powers seeking control of the West. The local land barons, empire-stealing cattle kings, and not to forget the common but ubiquitous outlaw who rules entire areas. Yet behind and beyond these men other enemies are active in the form of corrupt Washington politicians, giant railroad and mining interests, and wily land speculators who have usurped the settlers' land rights." Such flying buckshot made excellent copy, sold papers, but generally guaranteed a short life span for the editor.

He had seen the wall with the handwriting on it, and had quit, transferring his whole attention then to robbery under arms. It had been lucrative and, even better, exciting. Yet, there had been twinges of regret for the newspaper days. Charles Tisdale of Cambridge, Massachusetts, had disappeared into Butch Killigan, "The Terror of the Plains," as some clever editor had dubbed him; and the name had stuck. And even now, as he perused and sometimes carefully read rival papers to the *Declaimer*, he would come across that colorful sobriquet, and he would wonder in a strange, always vague way who he really was.

And now and again, in the lengthening evening as he wrote, and as he pondered, he wondered. Had he been blessed, or cursed? He found himself now sitting there at his desk with this question, looking down at the new and very blank sheet of paper upon which he had not yet continued writing his editorial, his thoughts having claimed him completely. And once again his fingers went to the scar and then began to feel over his whole face. And he remembered the photograph that was lying in the safe in a special folder, sealed with wax. The photograph of the young man at college, the young man with the interesting look in his eye. And he wondered again—as he did rarely—who he was, and who the young man in the photograph was. The photograph that he always refused to look at; and yet never threw away.

The knock at the door startled him. But recognition swiftly followed and he called, "Come."

"You look busy," Lily said. And then she added, "I hope I'm not interrupting you, or came too early or something." For he had looked startled, as though having been caught at something he shouldn't be doing.

And in fact that was how he felt; for indeed, he had been caught in his thoughts about the past.

"No," he said. "I was just working. And I am glad to see you. Just give me a minute or two while I wind this up." And he bent his head to his writing.

She sat quietly, looking about the room—at the printing press mostly, and also at the sheets of copy nailed onto the wall. She liked the smell of ink.

In only a few minutes he was finished and he put down his pen and looked at her. "How's it going down at the basin?"

"I'm close to ready. I can start maybe tomorrow."

"Good enough. That's the kind of news I want to hear."

She had walked across the room and now stood in front of him, her hands clasped lightly together in front of her, her head bent a little to one side; and there was a smile on her face.

"Did you ever run into a customer named Slocum?" he asked suddenly.

It startled her to have him talk of business, but only because she had been dreaming. "No. I don't always know the names though."

"Big man, black hair, got scars on his body I've been told. Green eyes. Women find him handsome."

She was searching. "No. I haven't. Most of what I meet ain't exactly what you'd call handsome." And then she was instantly blushing, her eyes dropping to the floor.

"Like me, huh?"

"No! No! Not like you! I ain't talking about that kind of—of handsome."

He watched the tears standing in her eyes. The light from the lamp caught them.

"I could always wear a mask to bed," he said.

And then suddenly she heard herself saying, "You'd better not, you ugly bastard!"

There was a moment then, a split instant when he felt something in himself, and somehow in some very strange way he felt her at the same time.

She was just standing there, her hand at her mouth, her eyes shining through her standing tears, as she looked at him steadily.

"Come here," he said. And his voice was quiet.

She always liked the smell of his breath when they were close together.

"Just two things," he said.

"Two?" And she was relieved at the quiet way he was speaking.

"Number one. If you ever hear of this man Slocum, or run into him, let me know immediately. Find out all you can, too. And let me know whatever right away."

"Sure."

He was silent.

"And what's the other thing?"

He didn't answer.

"Please tell me."

"I am—ugly," he said. "I—I got no kind of face." He said it simply, as though reading it from a book.

"I'd never noticed before that popped out. And I didn't mean it like you likely thought. I—I meant it like . . . I dunno. I dunno."

His voice now seemed to penetrate her as he spoke. "I know," he said. "I know how you meant it. And— and I reckon I'm . . ." He bit his lip and stood up suddenly. His voice was harder now, more his as he snapped at her, "You dumb shit. Go lock that door. And get your ass over here. I mean pronto!"

She was laughing as she hurried to the door, locked it, and ran back to where he was waiting by the horse-hair sofa.

Moments later as he was entering her he said, "You're what keeps me young."

She didn't speak. Her arms circled his head and she pulled him down and kissed him on his mouth. It was the first time.

After a while, Luther Bones and a man named Slim appeared and told them to come and eat. The marshal was of course limping along with his shotgun crutch, but he also had his gun hand close to his holstered Colt. His companion, to whom he referred as "Deputy Wall," held a cut-down shotgun in his hand, and had the look of a man who wanted to use it.

The two prisoners were marched into the marshal's office and told to sit. The marshal disappeared, leaving the deputy with them. Shortly, Bones was back, followed by a woman carrying a tray. She turned out to be his wife.

"Eat," she said, casting a glance at her husband, who was scowling, but also smelled of booze.

Slocum wondered if Deputy Wall had also been drinking. And his hopes lifted.

They ate in silence, which didn't take very long, since Bones kept telling them to hurry it up. And in a few moments they were back in their jail.

As he was leaving, Bones stopped and, looking right at Slocum, said, "Anything you got to say?"

"No."

"You don't want to confess?"

"Confess to what?"

"Murdering a man."

"What are you talking about? I hit him in his gun hand, where I aimed, dammit."

"He died."

"You're full of shit!"

"You are talking to the law, Slocum. Don't get sassy."

"Tell me what you really want, and let's cut the cackle."

The marshal took a step back, balancing himself easily with his shotgun. It was obvious he'd had a lot of practice. "Slocum, you are in big trouble. You wounded that feller, sure. But your bullet, after hitting his hand, then struck his gun barrel and ricocheted off and killed the man standing next to him. Shot him right through the heart. Slocum, you are in big, big trouble. I am holding you on the charge of murder. Now see how you can sass on that!"

Slocum was grinning. "That's a pretty good story, Marshal. Got to hand it to you. You beat them dime books they sell about how wild a place the West really is.''

For a moment he thought Bones wasn't going to say anything further. The man just stood there, leaning on his crutch with his head bent to one side.

"Deputy," he said, but speaking with his eyes still on Slocum. "You be witness to what I am telling this prisoner. The both of them. Anybody trying to excape from this here jail will be shot down like a dawg!''

And without another word he turned, almost spinning around on his crutch, and hobbled out of the log cabin. Deputy Wall followed, never taking his eyes off the prisoners, and with his shotgun at the ready.

"Funny," Sonny said, scratching his thick head of hair after the door closed and they heard the key turn in the lock.

Slocum looked at him. He was lying on his back on his bedding, with his hands behind his head.

"Funny as hell," he said.

"I mean funny that I come into town to find you so's to ask you to join up with us.''

"That's what I know.''

"Looks like you got joined up whether you wanted to or not," Sonny said.

"I am not joined up with you fellers, and I don't aim to be. I am a fellow minding his own business.''

"It looks like somebody else is trying to mind yours," Sonny observed.

"Mebbe.''

They were silent for some moments and then the young Kitchen spoke again. "You don't seem to mind much being stuck in this here jail with the prospect of maybe getting some of that famous frontier justice we're always hearing about.''

Slocum cut his eye at the boy now, who was standing in the center of the room with his hands in his hip pockets, regarding Slocum through lowered lids.

"We'll be out of here fair to soon now," Slocum said, and he rolled over and sat up.

Sonny's jaw had dropped open, his eyes had widened. "How d'you reckon?"

"Look. We were set up by those three. The one that came in last and shot from the door was the feller I backwatered out on the McGann range. All four were McGann men. Now, it could be that damn fool would want to dry-gulch me, but I doubt he'd really run such a risk, especially in a crowded saloon."

"You're saying that it was a fake!" Sonny Kitchen's eyes were like saucers.

"I am saying it was for sure set up by McGann to put me into a tight spot where he could talk business. I am also sure he didn't figure on you or somebody being with me. Still, the plan went through and here we are."

"Holy smokes!" Sonny took off his hat, scratched his head, and put his hat back on. "What's next then?"

"Mr. McGann is next," Slocum said, lying back and closing his eyes peacefully. "That's what's next."

"Holy shit!" Sonny Kitchen said those words with all the reverence of church prayer, and stared unbelieving at the man now sleeping soundly on the floor of the Landusky jail.

He always liked it whenever he walked into a saloon and there was that change in the atmosphere. It was the same now as he pushed back the swinging doors of the Elkhorn and walked in. It wasn't silence, it wasn't anything that obvious. But there was—as al-

ways—the different vibration. The action continued—the cards and dice, the table with the three-card
monte mechanic, the singsong of the faro dealer, the
whir of the wheel of fortune; even the screech and
squawk of the sawing fiddle coming through the open
door to the next room where the dancers cavorted—
only it was all different. He knew it like he knew the
razor edge of the Arkansas hunting knife he carried
in his boot. And it was good. And he knew too that
if it hadn't been that way, he would have had to make
it so. Indeed, he often did.

This day he drank at the bar, served carefully by
the big man with the thick fingers, the hidden eyes,
going under the name of Cornelius. But the Kid had
met him long ago. He hadn't been named Cornelius
then. Still, there was no sign of recognition passed
between them as the Kid said one word: "Whiskey."
And he didn't add that he wanted the good stuff and
not the leopard piss commonly known as trail whiskey. Such comment wasn't necessary. The sudden
flick of recognition in the big bartender's eyes had
said it all. And once again the Kid found himself. It
was worth it all, just for that moment of recognition,
of a pronouncement of his value.

He stood with his back to the room, but never with
his eyes away from the big mirror with the big crack
in it behind the bar.

He drank, and then the man going under the name
of Cornelius bought him another.

"Boss ain't around," he said, speaking low, and
only for the Kid's ears, which were bent at the tops
by his hat brim. "Case you wanted him."

"I only look for a man when he's in trouble," the
Kid said.

Color swept into Cornelius's long cheeks. "Sure."

But he remained where he was, wiping his hands on the apron that because of his strange girth was tied at his front with a tiny knot.

"Boss got a name?" the Kid asked after a while.

"Mr. Landusky. Thought you might be looking for him."

"He lookin' for me?"

"Not that I know of." Cornelius again wiped his hands on his apron. "Kid . . ."

And in that instant he was looking into two eyes that he would never forget, and his heart seemed to stop.

Mister . . . ," he said, trying to cover, but having trouble getting the word out.

"You got the name right this time. Don't forget it. It's 'Mister.' "

"Right."

"What's the boss's name again?"

"Landusky."

"That's the name of the town."

"Right."

"He own the town?"

"Pretty near."

"I thought McGann owned it."

Cornelius felt his palms go clammy again, and again he wiped them on the apron, then ran them along the sides of his trousers. He knew the Kid had no notion that McGann ran the town, so what was he up to?

"McGann don't run the town."

"What does he run?"

"Mostly the range from here to God knows where-all."

"Know a man name of Slocum?"

Later, Cornelius gave thanks to something or other—he wasn't sure what—that he'd caught the look in the Kid's bleak eye before denying such a knowledge. Fate, the Lord, Lady Luck—whoever— had intervened in the very split-nick of time.

"He is right now in Marshal Luther Bones's jail."

The Kid said nothing, revealed no sign of even having heard what the big bartender had said.

A moment or so passed and then Cornelius was called down to the other end of the bar. When he came back the atmosphere had lifted. The Kid was gone.

9

After drinking, though not heavily, at the Elkhorn, the Kid had moved across the street to the Jarnegan House—a huge, sprawling saloon, gambling parlor, and dance hall that had been built during the last year of the War Between the States by Tully Jarnegan, a man from the Old Country who had come close to the heavyweight championship of the ring, but just before his big fight with Yankee Sullivan he'd been thrown from a lumber wagon when his foot missed the brake. The wagon had rammed the horses, the team bolted, and the wagon wheels ran over Tully Jarnegan's legs.

When the scenery at the Jarnegan House grew tiresome, the Kid crossed the street to the Jolly Wizard Hotel, a rip-roaring, hell-for-leather saloon run by Clayton Cuff, a gent who claimed to have been chef to the crowned heads of Europe and some of the richest men in New York and Boston. But in his present capacity those talents he had brought with him were hardly necessary. The Jolly Wizard was famous not for its cuisine, but for its wild shenanigans. Those shenanigans were brought by a clientele consisting in the main of trail-honed cowhands, outlaws, gamblers and toughs and others of ill repute.

For a change the Jolly Wizard was quiet. Outside in the street the afternoon was also quiet; and the Kid, leaning against the bar drinking casually, surveyed the room with a practiced, professional eye. And for a change there weren't many customers in the room. He was wondering what the man McGann had hired him to watch was doing in jail. And he assumed his arrest must have been quite recent, since McGann had not mentioned the fact of his having been arrested. But he would see. Meanwhile, he was waiting for Collie and the boys to find him. He had told them to meet him in town. It was up to them to find where he was. But he expected them this day. The Newcastle holdup had gone off without a hitch, exactly as planned, and he was pleased to see that the boys were alert and able to follow his orders, and even improvising when it was necessary. It had been a training run really, though it had brought in good money. Yet, the main thing had been to see what kind of shape the five were in. Because he was going to need them for the Big Thing.

And interestingly, the Big Thing had fallen right into his hands; right out of the clouds, by God! Who would have imagined something working out so easily, with such coincidence! Out of the blue, McGann offering him a job to watch the very man he'd been looking for. Out of the blue, the rancher paying him big money to do just what he was planning to do anyway.

He wasn't fooled by McGann. The rancher had

hired him to watch Slocum, but he knew very well what that meant to one of those cattle barons. He knew he was actually getting hired to kill the man—or would be. Nothing had been said, but McGann had set Slocum in the small cattlemen's camp. That was enough right there to sign the man's death warrant. But of course when he got orders from McGann to kill, he would up his price. He would have leverage then. And he would get the nice money for doing what was his great pleasure to do. Kill John Slocum!

Slocum had been lying on his bedding half-awake, when he heard the key in the padlock.

"Somebody!" Sonny Kitchen's hasty whisper seemed almost a shout in the cabin.

Slocum said nothing. He cleared his throat so that young Kitchen would know he was awake. Then he turned his face halfway toward the door, his eyes slitted so that he could see, though appearing to be asleep.

It was again Luther Bones and his deputy.

"You men wake up!"

Slocum opened his eyes. He heard Sonny stir. He didn't look at his horologe, but figured the time by the light at the open doorway, judging it to be around noon. He was lying on his back with his hands at his belt buckle, ready just in case physical action became necessary.

"Come on, Sonny. Somebody's put up bail for you. I dunno why."

"Bail?"

Slocum had warned him that something like this could happen; that they'd be separated, and they had worked out a provisional plan. He was pleased at the tone of surprise Sonny had managed at the marshal's announcement.

"Who put up the bail, Marshal?" Slocum suddenly asked. "I don't reckon it was yourself nor your deputy there."

"That ain't your business, Slocum." Luther Bones was glaring at him. "That's Kitchen here I am talkin' to."

"Who put it up?" Sonny said, his voice calm, but with a quick look in Slocum's direction.

"This ain't the place to talk about that," Bones said, sharp.

"I just bet it was Mr. Tom McGann," Slocum said, and suddenly he was sitting up on his bedding, looking hard at the marshal and his deputy. And he noted the surprise hitting into the marshal's shoulders as he caught him off guard. Bones had his back to him and now he turned, composing himself. But Slocum knew he had the setup right on the line.

"Well, for a gut, Slocum, he ain't puttin' up any bail for yerself."

The remark, spoken so tightly, coupled with the shifty look in the lawman's face, told Slocum what he wanted to know. It indeed was McGann who was springing young Kitchen. It was all happening just the way he'd told the boy it would. He just hoped that Sonny would follow the plan he'd laid out—to do nothing. Not to argue, but to let them let him go; and ride on home.

In the next minute the door was closed, the padlock was snapped and Slocum was alone. It was clear to him now that the setup wasn't going to include Sonny, and maybe not even the Kitchens, but himself. He had no firm reason for thinking that, yet he felt it strongly. Felt it with that sense of certainty that he always trusted. And in about an hour when he heard the key again in the padlock he knew he was right.

Again it was Bones and Deputy Wall.

"You've got company, Slocum. Don't worry, it ain't the circuit judge."

"Didn't figure it was, Marshal, I'd just hoped it was some nice person who was going to spring me out of here, providing I'd do just what he wanted." And he grinned a big grin at Bones as he stood in the center of the room with his hands on his hips, while the lean, tobacco-chewing cattleman—for he couldn't have been anything else—stepped into the cabin.

"I'm Tom McGann."

"What can I do for you, McGann?"

Slocum's tone of voice had not been hard, but it hadn't been friendly either. He had decided to take the initiative. The stockman cleared his throat and half turned toward the two lawmen, with a slight nod.

When they were gone, McGann walked over to the stove, which was not in use, lifted the lid, and spat a great gob of brown and yellow tobacco juice inside. Then he replaced the lid. Canting his head at Slocum he said, "Don't want to mess up this nice clean jail, do I?"

But Slocum had already decided on how he was going to play his hand, and it didn't include his picking up on the humor. He said nothing.

McGann shifted his weight, reassessing the situation somewhat. "I've come to make you an offer, Slocum."

"I have got nothing else to do but listen. Right now it 'pears to me you're the only game in town."

A hard grin flashed across the cattleman's face at that, but vanished almost before it registered. Slocum didn't take it as a friendly gesture, but something quite automatic. It gave him an insight into McGann's nature, all the same.

"You're in a jam, Slocum." McGann held up his hand even before he finished his sentence, anticipating an objection. But Slocum wasn't even about to speak. He knew what was coming, and he could tell that McGann knew he knew.

"You'd be cooped in here for one helluva long time, near as I can figger from what Bones has to say," McGann went on. "But my offer might be something you could listen to."

He paused, chewing again, releasing the bulge in his cheek where he'd parked his chew in order to speak. Again he walked to the stove, lifted the lid and shot a wad right into the cold cavern, and replaced the lid.

"I could use a man like yerself. You more'n likely know I got a range war on my hands, could explode any minute. Me and the other stockgrowers in this country have got to see to it that the peace is kept. Hell, you're a man of experience—I have heard about you—an' you know what such a thing can do to everybody. Tears everything and everybody apart! I am trying to keep peace and get them knotheaded men to talk to each other. Now . . ."

He paused, putting one leg forward, like a horse, Slocum thought, getting ready to bend down and rub his nose against it. He kept the stance and brought up his hands in front of him and began ticking off his points on his thick, stubby fingers.

"Now, number one, some of them small stockgrowers'll listen to me on account of I bin here longest than anybody, and also I ain't gonna bullshit them. I am talkin' about the honest ones, not them sonsofbitches who bin throwing their goddam running irons

on my beef. But the ones that got some sense and
decency about theirselves. They'll listen to me, on
account of they know I will talk straight to them, like
I said, but also—number two—on account of I got
the men to police the country against any more rus-
tling. See, those small outfits also get their stock rustled. They seem to fergit about that. They get their
beeves stolen just like the rest of us. On account of
the rustlers operating out of the box canyon country
up there on the north fork, with that feller Use Moriarty. You heerd of him?''

Slocum nodded.

"Then you know he is one slick sonofabitch. Like
you know, Slocum, the rustlers get wind of range
trouble and they collect like flies, playing one side
agin the other, stealin' stock right and left, and robbing all round. What I am getting at is—''

"You want a range detective, a regulator,'' Slocum
said, cutting him off neat. "Number three—right?''

McGann nodded.

"Funny how I figured that's what you were about
with those four guns in the saloon.''

"I dunno what you're talking about.''

"Cut it out, McGann. I'll give your offer a couple
of throws, but just cut horseshittin' me. I don't like
it.'' He stood square in front of the cattleman with
his thumbs hooked into his belt, looking straight where
his words were hitting.

McGann nodded. "Good enough then. We'll go
pick up your weapons. Then we'll talk some more.''

"I am a man of few words, McGann. And I use
them few damn seldom.''

This time McGann did let the grin come out. But
it wasn't the friendly kind. Rather it was an appre-
ciation, Slocum felt, of one wolf for another. Well—

good enough, by God. And as he left the little jail he felt good. He'd no notion of what he was getting into, but he still felt good.

In the marshal's office he picked up his guns—the Colt and his Winchester, which they'd taken from his saddle boot. And followed McGann out into the street.

"We'll have us a drink at the Elkhorn. I want people to see us together."

Meanwhile, Slocum's mind was racing. The plan, of course, was amazingly simple. By his presence with McGann at the Elkhorn he was giving notice to everybody that he was riding on the big stockgrowers' side. But at the same time McGann was no dumbbell. He had to know that a man of the kind he'd figured himself to be wouldn't go for that kind of thing. McGann, unless he was a deaf, dumb, and blind fool, couldn't possibly believe that he would agree to those terms; that he would turn on the Kitchens, for instance, and help the big cowmen.

As they made their way into the Elkhorn, slapping open the batwing doors, Slocum wondered just how far McGann would push; trying to use him as a figurehead. The man had to know he was friendly with the Kitchens, otherwise what was he doing with Sonny Kitchen in the saloon? And besides, he could easily have been seen riding around the Kitchens' spread when he'd scouted the area. So what was it? He suddenly felt that he was being set up in a certain way. The reasons that McGann had told him for getting him out of jail—which he'd clearly set up in the first place—were full of holes. He was being set up for something else. But why? McGann didn't even know him. It was pointing then toward someone else setting him up through McGann; and that meant McGann in turn had somebody else squeezing him.

Who?

By the time they reached the Elkhorn, Slocum had come to the conclusion that McGann just had to be working with somebody else, or he was making a deal with somebody else—one; or maybe both.

Well, at least he was out of that damn jail; an easy next step had he remained would of course have been a raid, leading to a lynching. Somebody was damn eager for his blood. But who? He didn't know anybody in this part of the country. Hadn't been through here in years. So—who? Who had it in for him bad enough to kill; especially with such elaborate planning?

The plan, as told to Slocum by McGann, was marvelously simple. The big stockmen would round up their herds and drive them up to the higher country for summer grazing.

"It should be a simple operation," McGann pointed out. "We will alert all the outfits that are in the way that we will be coming through. We don't want anyone to get hurt, but it is our graze not only on the mountain, but through the whole north end of the basin."

"You're saying then that what you're going to do, McGann, is run your cattle right through about four of the spreads between yourself and the mountain feed. Instead of going around by Wood River, you'll take that shortcut right through Hardwater Basin."

Slocum said it clear and hard, looking right into the cattleman's lined face.

"You got it right, mister." McGann spoke no less hard than Slocum.

"I am one man, McGann. I sure as hell can't guarantee you success. Those stockgrowers are going to fight you right down to the last bullet.''

"Then we will have to defend ourselves, Slocum.''

Slocum studied it. He'd suspected something tricky, but not this bad.

"You call moving all that cattle through somebody else's range defending yourself!''

"That's the only way we can look at it.''

"Not we, McGann. You.''

They had been sitting at a table having a drink near the far end of the room, away from the bar, and now Slocum sat back, letting his hands fall to his knees, as though preparing to get up.

"Where you going?'' McGann said. "Back to jail? Or with me?'' And he nodded toward the swinging doors, on each side of which a man was standing, apparently idling, yet the six-guns were each in clear view in their holsters. "You can't outdraw them both, Slocum. They're too far apart.'' McGann reached to his shirt pocket and pulled out a packet of tobacco, ready for a fresh chew. "Listen, Slocum. Those two will be covering you while you're working for—or let's say with—me.''

"And what are you figuring for me to do?''

A kind of grin came into Tom McGann's eyes at that point. Except that there was no humor in it that Slocum could see.

"What I want you to do,'' McGann said. And he paused, as though collecting himself, not just what he wanted to say. And the fleeting moment struck Slocum in a strange way; something quite different—even alien, Slocum thought—had come into the cattleman. Even his voice had a different resonance as he said, "It might be I'll want you to kill a man.''

Tom McGann sat there, still holding his packet of chewing tobacco. A moment passed, and then he reached into his pocket and took out his knife and carved a slice and popped it into his mouth.

The moment passed, and McGann was again Tom McGann. While Slocum studied the two gunmen at the door.

"You could get away, Slocum," McGann said. "I wouldn't want to have them shoot up the place; a lot of people here. But they'll be on your trail. Night and day."

"McGann, I don't hire my gun. You damned fool. Couldn't you tell that?"

"You're saying you don't kill except somebody comes at you."

"You got it."

"Then that's what I bin sayin'!"

"You're saying the man you want me to kill is also figuring to kill me. That it?"

"That's the size of it."

Slocum felt his anger rising, but he let it go. It was no time for anger. Definitely not the time for blowing off.

"You going to tell me who?"

"I've done what I could, Slocum." The cattleman paused then, as though listening to himself. "All I've said to you is I want you to work with me. You side with those Kitchens and the others, you're buying big trouble. Heap big trouble!"

"But this feller, he wants to kill me anyway, is that it?"

"I'll just say one thing. I don't go for killing either, Slocum. Like yourself, I kill in self-defense, when I got to. I don't go for gunmen, though when the going gets tough a man's got to get tough himself. Can't argue that one."

"This man knows me?"

McGann nodded. "I do believe so."

"Tell me who he is then."

"I don't know his name. He was sent to me. I don't want him. I know the type. Back killer."

"Then why don't you get rid of him?"

"That is what I want you to do," the rancher said, and Slocum watched the grayness coming in around his eyes.

A long moment passed. Slocum was watching the men at the door. He was convinced McGann didn't want a shooting in the saloon.

"Do you know why this bugger wants to gun me?"

"I don't. But I wouldn't be surprised if he wanted to build his rep by adding a notch to his gun."

"The old story," Slocum said softly, almost speaking to himself, and he added, "and the new."

He turned now and faced McGann squarely. Was the man lying? Normally, under ordinary circumstances, he would have said no; he would have given McGann the benefit of the doubt. But he could see the man was under pressure. He was into something right up to his ears, and someone was pouring it on him. For a moment he remembered Jillie McGann, realizing with a shock that this was her father. A man hooked up with a crazy killer, was the way it read; trying to euchre himself—Slocum—into getting the load off him.

He stood up, and waited, his knuckles lightly touching the rim of the round table as he looked straight at Tom McGann.

"I don't want any part of you, McGann. All I can say to you is, you got trouble with somebody, you straighten it out. Don't try to euchre me into settling your problems. And next to that I will be riding with the Kitchens."

"I can still have you thrown back in jail, Slocum."

"Except you won't."

He waited a beat as he saw the cattleman move his head in a negative with his eyes on the men at the door.

"I'm letting you out of this one, Slocum. Like I said, I don't want to mess up Cornelius's saloon. But you side with those goddam Kitchens you're fair game."

Slocum said nothing as he turned and strode toward the doors that led to the street.

As he drew close to the two toughs he watched them move apart. Either they were ignoring McGann's signal, which wasn't likely, or the rancher had given them a new signal from where Slocum couldn't see him.

Slocum was within just a few feet of them when suddenly he moved off to his left, but he was only feinting and in the next instant he'd peeled to his right, grabbed the nearest gunman, and had his arm twisted up behind his back, so hard the man cried out. But Slocum had him from behind and now used him as a shield as the other gunslinger charged him. He waited just a second and then shoved his captive right at the other man, kicking him in back of his knee as he did so. The gunman let out a shriek of pain, and Slocum watched as his companion staggered with the force of the body that had been shoved right into him.

The second man now made the mistake of reaching for his gun. But Slocum had his Colt out and up and slammed him alongside the jaw with the gun barrel.

Then he was out in the street, as cries of outrage followed him from the saloon. But no one came out in person.

Swiftly, he made it down to the livery and led the

Appaloosa out into the corral. The late-afternoon sunlight was drenching the town as he bridled the horse and then saddled him. No one had come after him.

A minute later he was in the saddle and riding out of town. And as he rode quickly down the trail he told himself that there was still time to really decide what he was going to do. He could still head for the north country, or even west. There would be plenty of work about for an able hand. It would be good to get at some work again. Cow or horse stuff.

He found that thought still in his mind as he turned the Appaloosa onto the trail that would lead him to Hardwater Basin and the Kitchen spread.

10

"You want another, Tom?"

It was Cornelius, standing there, wiping his pointed hands in the greasy, damp apron he wore around his great girth.

McGann looked up, his face dark, wrinkled around his eyes, and he moved his jaws slowly, activating his chew, which he'd forgotten about.

Seeing it was Cornelius, he nodded.

Cornelius belched softly as he poured a generous amount into Tom McGann's glass, and added some of his own, which he had carried over from the bar. Looking up he caught the eye of Nick, the other bartender on duty, and nodded. It was time for a break.

The room had resumed instantly after the action between Slocum and the two Double Box men. Such physical dispute was not uncommon. Nor did Cornelius mind too much, except when the place was wrecked. After all, the level of excitement was what kept customers coming. Of course, it had been close just now, for he'd not been sure but that the Double Box three might start throwing lead instead of punches. But of course Slocum had been onto it too.

"That's a pretty tough boy there, wouldn't you say?" Cornelius, addressing the top of McGann's head, sat down.

"Huh." The rancher's shoulders lifted and dropped as he gave a sort of grunt. "You want to know something, Corn? I will tell you, by God it was a whole helluva lot easier fightin' Looking Horse and his Arapahoes than fer Chrissakes wrangling this fuckin' bunch of cows an' men and hosses that I bin doin' since those screaming, murderin' savages—as the newspaper fellers calls 'em—was pulling their depredations all over the hell and gone of this here country. I mean what I am sayin'!"

A rich, confiding chuckle rumbled out of the barkeeper's loose lips. "The good old days," he said. "May they never come back."

And even the doleful McGann raised his head for a chuckle at that.

"You always got a job with me, Tom." It was a joke they'd shared for a number of years, but now the cattleman didn't think it so funny. He simply grunted. "Tom . . ."

"That is sure as the Lord made little apples my name, Corn. Exceptin' sometimes I dunno but what I might be somebody else. Jesus!"

They chuckled softly at that, without mirth, but more in recognition of a friendship that neither would have named as such. Now a silence claimed them, wrapping even the table and their drinks along with them in a sort of solitude in the midst of the raucous merriment that even in the few quiet moments could yet be heard, as though in echo.

Then in a low voice, the bartender said, "You know he was in here. I couldn't believe it."

McGann raised his head and looked straight at Cornelius, who was slowly moving his pointed head with its slicked-down wet black hair from side to side.

"Him?"

"Him."

"Jesus . . ." The name fell absently from the cattleman's mouth as though unrecognized, more careless than if he'd been remarking simply on the weather.

And yet Cornelius knew him for a religious man. Strange, for the fact was that he himself was absolutely without any religion or faith in The Above; yet he would not have said the name with that lifelessness. Or, he wondered, was it simply familiarity? Cornelius was a quarter Atsina, though it was not known to anyone except his wife, a white woman, and Tom McGann, a white man. Indeed, between Cornelius and McGann it was a desperate secret. For no Indian would ever have been allowed even to work in a saloon let alone own one. But the quarter Atsina knew that it was such a secret that held people together, that could create a bond that mere friendship, which was so often unreliable, could not offer.

"Where did you see him?" McGann asked now.

"Right here. He walked in cool as a whistle and bought a drink."

"Did he know you knew him?"

"Dunno."

McGann didn't speak and so a silence fell between them.

Then Cornelius said, "I'd say you seen him."

"And you'd be betting your whole pot on it."

"Did he look you up?"

"No. Somebody sent him. I needed a tough ram-rodder for the situation coming up. Real tough. And I—I asked about, and somebody came through with himself."

"He could just as easy walk in here right now," Cornelius said, cutting his eyes to the swinging doors, which for the moment were in repose.

"Well, it's been a while since he killed Blount. Can't say I miss Blount. But he did be pretty fair to straight."

"He shotgunned him, I'd heard," Cornelius said.

"I was the one who found him." McGann reached for his drink. "His head looked like a busted apple. His whole body did. He gave him two blasts of them blue whistlers."

"Not necessary," Cornelius said, resorting to whiteman Indian jargon. "One load enough. Even one bullet. I heard he was near cut in two and then shot in the head."

"Correct," said McGann. "That was the way of it."

"Now you got him."

McGann nodded. "Like I said, he was sent. I need a tough man. And I guess—yes, I got him." McGann looked at Cornelius then; until then he'd been talking with his eyes mostly on the table that they were leaning on. But now he looked at the barkeep.

"I got him and I'm in a tight," he said, looking down at his hands.

"Somebody is squeezing you, I can tell."

"It's hard to hide."

"You're doing all right. I notice things most people mostly don't see. Generally, I forget what I see right now. My dad was a riverboat gambler an' he mostly raised me. I think he done a good job."

"You've handled a tough business, I'd say," McGann said, coming out of his shell a bit.

"You treated me good a long way back," Cornelius said suddenly. "I always figured I owed you, see. So remember that. What the hell, I got my secrets too."

McGann nodded.

"Course, the trouble with secrets is it's always the wrong people finds out about 'em."

A wry smile touched the corners of the rancher's mouth as Cornelius finished speaking. "You know something, Corn; if I had it to do over I'd still hold up that goddam bank. Let me tell you one thing. In those days it was fun. And hell, it was that job that got me the money to git started." He paused. "Only thing is Jillie. I don't want her finding out."

"That is how the little sonofabitch is twisting you, huh?"

"That's how."

They were silent for a few moments, and then McGann said, "I just can't get the sight of Blount out of my head. Jesus, all the poor bastard did was write one of his editorials saying we ought to clean up the country from the road agents and horse thieves and such. He was just doing what any of them newspapermen do."

"You're talking about the way Blount was killed."

"Yes, the way. Two loads of buckshot. It couldn't have been a more painful way of expanding a man into nothing. In other words, blowing him to hell, or maybe to heaven. Who knows . . ." He paused, shaking his head slowly.

"There is just one thing I am worried about," McGann said.

Cornelius knew that he was expected to say something here, but he couldn't think of anything, and so he simply said, "Huh . . ."

They were silent, but then Cornelius thought of something. "You could send your daughter away for a while," he said.

"I spoke to her about that and she refused. Flat! Said she wouldn't even think of it!"

"Sounds like maybe she had got some boyfriend around somewheres."

"I worry about her," McGann said. "I worry about her a lot. I don't want that little sonofabitch even *thinking* about her!"

"I wouldn't either," Cornelius said.

McGann was shaking his head slowly, his thoughts still in the past. "Sometimes I think of Blount, see what that little sonofabitch done to him. Maybe I'm gettin' old, but that bastard! Two loads like that. He's a goddam animal!"

"No," Cornelius said. "No, he ain't no animal. A animal don't do a thing like that. I got to tell you, Tom. That's the way the whites lie. See, a animal didn't do it, but you call him a animal. A animal didn't. A man did it. A white man."

He had been well aware of Tom McGann watching his set-to with his two men. The encounter was over with almost immediately, and he'd been just waiting for the cattleman to pull something on him. But he had noted earlier that McGann wasn't packing a handgun, at least not in view. He was—no doubt about it—one of those tough old boys like Shanghai Pierce and Jesse Chisholm and the like who disdained handguns; considering themselves too important to resort to lowly combat of that nature. Of course, that didn't eliminate their use of other men to do the dirty work, as indeed McGann had wanted himself to do.

Still, he was watching his backtrail carefully. McGann was clearly in some kind of tight and so might do something quite unexpected to force his hand.

And then—without the least warning, or even thought—but with the suddenness of a flash storm, there she was. Sitting a sorrel horse with a flaxen mane and tail and three white stocking feet.

He couldn't have been more surprised if she'd suddenly dropped out of a cloud. And pleased! But quickly throwing himself on guard, for he knew how foolishness with a woman at such a time as this gets more men in trouble that anything a man could imagine.

There she was at the side of the trail, sitting alert in the same roping saddle, the same bridle with the spade bit, but a different horse. All of that went into him in a flash, without even thought interfering. An instant impression, along with all the rest—her sapphire blue riding shirt, tight jodhpurs, and her brown hair, low over her eyes, which were again shining directly at him.

"I was hoping I would run into you!" And she gave a little shy laugh.

"Well, you could knock me down with a singletree," he said. "You're the last one I'd have expected to run into out here—but I am real glad to see you."

"Mr. Slocum, you know how to deal the charm," she said, without taking her eyes from him.

"It ain't charm, miss; it's only that any fool could see that you're the only thing about that's better looking than the country."

"Thank you, sir."

"You got a minute? You mind if I build myself a smoke?"

"Would you show me how?" She was suddenly like a little girl, all eagerness at learning and playing.

"Thing is not to lay on too much tobacco," he said.

And as he pulled the drawstring on his tobacco sack with his teeth, she said, "I see two hands aren't enough."

He grinned. "Then you roll it like this, lick it." And he ran the open edge of the paper along the tip of his tongue, then twisted the end of his smoke and licked it; all in one easy, unbroken movement, and the cigarette was in his mouth. "Done!"

"I will have to practice that. But I don't want to take up your time now."

She seemed to him to be a little out of breath.

"I don't reckon I want to take up yours," he said.

"I've got all the time in the world. But I know you don't. My father said he might be seeing you. I overheard him telling one of the men as I came into the room. But I don't know if he did; and it's not my business—but, all the same, I was hoping I'd run into you on my way to town."

"To see your dad?"

She nodded. "Is he all right?"

"Seemed to be."

"Ah—good."

"Hasn't he been well?"

"No, he's all right. But a bit off his feed, I'd say, to use one of his expressions. He's got a lot on his mind I guess, with roundup and all that."

"He seemed fine to me," Slocum said, wondering how much she knew, but figuring it couldn't be much.

McGann looked like the sort of man who wouldn't confide his business to his daughter.

"Well, I won't keep you if you're getting on to town," he said.

"I don't want to keep you." And then she gave a little laugh. "Except, to be honest with you, I really do. I've got some coffee in my pack. It wouldn't take a minute." And she looked at him with an expression of absolutely pure innocence. Slocum felt his heart bounce.

"I can't," he said. And then, suddenly dropping his eyes, he squinted at the sorrel pony. "Horse looks like he's got something in his shoe."

"He has been walking a bit funny. I was about to get down and take a look when I saw you coming," she said.

Slocum was already out of the saddle and had lifted the sorrel's left foreleg, and was examining the shoe.

"Got a stone there, pushing on his frog," he said. "The shoe ain't loose. I can get that out, I believe."

He let the horse have his leg back and reached into his pocket for his clasp knife. Then he picked up the leg again, the sorrel standing easy with the girl still in the saddle, and working quickly, but not hurrying, he extracted the stone.

"There you go, boy." And he gave the horse a pat on the shoulder.

She had climbed down and was now standing beside him. "Thanks for that. That was very nice of you. I am very lucky that you happened along."

Slocum said nothing. He was standing there, with his hand still on the sorrel's shoulder, looking at the girl.

"Coffee?" she asked. "I'm not worried now about

my horse getting lame and I wouldn't get to town. I thank you again.''

In the next moment they were in each other's arms. Slocum was instantly thankful that he'd had the presence of mind to have already moved with her into the shelter of some trees off the side of the trail. When they lay down they were well protected from any one riding by.

Hungrily they removed their clothes and were now lying totally naked as she guided his rigid organ into her soft, eager vagina.

''I want you . . .'' She gasped the words as he drove deep into her, and she spread her legs wider.

He had a breast in his mouth, and she had reached down to hold both his balls as they began slowly to pump together.

''It's delic—delicious,'' she murmured, hardly able to speak. But they did not interrupt any of it in order to be more articulate. Their bodies did the talking, the loving, the gasping and thrusting and squeezing, and finally the great coming. ''I want him . . . I want him . . . I want him . . . ,'' she was gasping as Slocum drove deep into her, rubbing the head of his erection up against her wall while she wiggled and stroked, drawing him totally as they came squirting together in one totality, one bliss. . . .

''No one will deny that the depredations of the 'outlaw element' in and around Hardwater Basin and for a wide area around—at all points of the compass—have reached such proportions that stagger the imagination, and that ere long must finally stir the attention of the army at Fort Madison, and indeed the very seat of government as far away as Washington. Yet time is of the essence and it is for all humble and concerned citizens to be thankful that Tom McGann—along with his loyal men—has issued a firm warning to the rustlers, horse thieves, highwaymen, and all other ilk of nefarious and outright dangerous characters who have for too long preyed upon the honest citizens—the cattlemen, the townsfolk, the humble and glorious pioneers of our Great Western Territory. The time has come for us to gird our loins and rid ourselves forever of these fractious and violent elements. Peaceful means have not prevailed, though Tom McGann has insisted on 'the way of the Law and the Lord,' and has himself followed both the laws of man and the laws of God with equal vigor. The *Declaimer* and all its readers and future readers must bring just claim to their own efforts to support Tom McGann and his— yes! his holy enterprise! EVIL—GET THEE AWAY FROM GOD'S LAND AND GOD'S CHILDREN!''

Hot damn—that was telling them! The editor, publisher, and principal writer of the *Rocky Mountain Declaimer* read the front-page editorial again, and felt yet once more the stirring in his breast that those vigorous words brought.

He had run off a large overrun and had hired extra riders to deliver the paper to the far reaches of the country—north to Little Fork, south to Horn Butte, and east and west until the deliverers ran out of newspapers.

Faithful ''reporters,'' serving the *Declaimer* as eyes, ears, and voices spreading the news verbally— as per directions of their editor—also added enthusiasm and energy to the great enterprise that Miles Landusky had launched. He of course realized—well versed as he was in the weaknesses of men—that word of mouth was his best channel to the prejudices, beliefs, and fears of citizens within the *Declaimer*'s circle of influence.

Miles Landusky, formerly Butch Killigan, formerly Charles Tisdale—a "man of parts," even if he did say so himself—sat now in his office, not only the headquarters of the *Declaimer* but the hub for his Great Enterprise—the final effort that would lead him to the office of representative of the territory.

He reached to the desk now—he was sitting only an arm's length away—and took hold of the bottle of bourbon whiskey and poured some into his glass.

Ah, that was good. His thoughts, fresh as the dawn, played on his achievement thus far. He had McGann in line, and he had Use Moriarty working quite under his direction out of the box canyons—preying on stages, trains, travelers, and even a bank. Moriarty and his lieutenants wreaked havoc on the surrounding trails—robbing mine shipments, and miners, and of course Wells Fargo and other shippers with equal zeal and effect.

Use Moriarty, being most adroit at planning and at killing and at executing precise plans, was considered the head or chief of the half dozen bandit gangs that holed up and raided out of the box canyons up north of town. It was a beautiful situation—with himself as Miles Landusky, the stalwart purveyor of the people's voice; the standard of morality, honesty, and good common sense; publishing that great organ of news and perception as to what was going on in the country around the mining camps and ranches in the northern part of the territory. Indeed, a standard-bearer with a town named after him. And now ready for his final step to unaccountable power in the territory. Though not forgetting some old scores to settle along the way.

He took a drink. It was good after this long and

bitter time to be able to see success lying right before him.

The combination of Moriarty, the epitome of what a road agent needed to be—he was everything!—and Tom McGann, the rugged western cattleman building the West. The black and white of it, it could be put, was a situation in which he—Landusky—provided the balance. And with the provoking and the eventual explosion and then the solution of the "grazing problem," the water rights, the fencing, and all the rest of it, pitting one against the other—the night riders against the law, the big stockgrowers against the small cattlemen, the cattlemen against the swarms of immigrants, farmers, sodbusters; with his great ability to take advantage of men's weaknesses, through the greed of the landgrabbers, the pious avarice of the speculators for the railroad, with so many against and so many afraid, each longing for something; why, it was the simplest thing in the world for the man with the cool head, the steady eye, the firm hand to manipulate—greed against greed, fear against fear—and so to rule by division.

Plus of course the great joy in the excitement, the great fun in all the bullshit. As he sat there now, fondling his glass, he thought back to those pranks at school and college that were so inventive, so exciting, and such great fun! The time he'd issued a hundred invitations to a party at the Reverend Osgood Smithers's mansion knowing through private information that the Reverend was to be away on that particular day. And then the time he and his gang of anywhere from two to a dozen—as the spoof dictated—dug a hole right in the middle of Boston, putting up signs that they were digging a foundation for an English ambassador's new home. But then, with the huge hole almost complete, they'd disappeared, leaving the hole. What pranks! He chuckled now recalling the excitement of those halcyon days. Well, by golly, they were going to come again. But first he was going to do two things. Number one, see that the small cattlemen were crushed so that he could buy land, using McGann to the hilt. Number two, which actually might be simultaneous with the land acquisition, would be his appointment as representative for the territory. But then, there was a third—not that he'd forgotten it, but it was so wonderfully unique he hadn't wanted to think of it as a "third" part, say on an isosceles triangle. And he chuckled at his former education in geometry. Number three was, and of course, the big surprise. Number three was the game that would settle his role as the Great Peacemaker, the man who ended the awesome reign of the highwaymen and killers whose depredations had come within a flicker of bringing the whole Northwest to its knees. And it would be dramatized in settling the hash of the little sonofabitch with that goddam drop of water on the end of his beak!

When the knock came at the door of his office, Miles Landusky released a great sigh. A man always given to self-dramatization, he heard that knock as the signal for the start of his big push. And so he all but shouted, "Come!"

And indeed, as he had expected, it was Tom McGann; sturdy, grim-faced, and obviously resolved about something or other. They had planned to meet, to go through the final touches in case anything had to be changed.

"I take it you are ready to go," Landusky said,

reaching to his box of cigars, taking one, and then offering one to McGann.

"I am ready," McGann said. "The boys have started pulling in the herd, and counting head."

"And as far as you figure no one's spilled anything on it. That right?"

"No one I know of. And if anybody has, and I find out who it is, I'll cut him right off at the kneecaps."

McGann was not joking, he was dead serious; in sharp contrast to the good spirits Landusky was showing.

"You'll start pushing them through the basin tomorrow morning."

"First crack of dawn a thousand head will be on their way. There'll be follow-up. I've got another team rounding up after these here get moving."

"Good work. No trouble, eh?"

"Naw . . . well, nothing I could say was trouble." He reached to the box of cigars that Landusky had pushed forward.

But Landusky was on him like a hawk. "There is something, McGann. Better tell me what it is."

A stab of irritation ran through the cattleman. He hated that arrogance in Landusky, but he was in no position to throw anything away by straightening the ugly bastard out.

"Better tell me what it is, Tom. We can't afford to have anything kinky in the operation." Landusky took a drag on his cigar, his eyes—or at any rate, his good one—on the other man. "It's the Kid, is it." Saying it as a statement and not a question, it left no out for McGann to deny it without an effort he didn't want to give.

He sighed.

"Man's there. Use him, Tom."

"I told you I didn't want him. I took one look at him, and even though something said I ought to have a tough gun, a real tough gun, in my pack, there was something about that little sonofabitch . . . I dunno. I'm for dropping him. I can't trust him. I just got that feeling the man has got something else going at the same time he's supposed to be working for me."

"For us," Landusky corrected.

Even while he was speaking Landusky was shaking his head. McGann was about to tell him to cut it out or else, but once again he remembered it was no time to be foolish.

"Tom, you keep him. Use him. We both can use him. You understand . . ." And there was just a tinge of iron in his voice now as he leaned forward onto his desk, stabbing the air in front of him with his thick forefinger. "You remember when we made our agreement, especially your end of the deal!"

"I do. But the Kid was not in the picture then."

"But I was. And I am now. And the agreement was that I would overlook—uh—a certain something that I just happened to be aware of in your—past—and you would follow my directions. Am I right, Tom? Tom, have I got it straight? Tell me if I'm wrong. Tell me. I mean, now, tell me if I misunderstood you, Tom."

McGann was all but grinding his teeth in rage and frustration, and Landusky could hardly keep from breaking out into laughter. His red, leering face seemed to shine at the stockgrower, who felt quite as though he were hamstrung.

Which he was, Landusky was thinking at exactly that moment. The poor sonofabitch was hamstrung. Well, tough titty. Tough. He would do exactly what he was told to do, and that included keeping the Kid right where he could find him.

He stood up then, the cigar clamped in his teeth, his fingers bent, so that his knuckles touched the edge of his desk.

"You've arranged for riders to keep me posted."

"I have." Reluctantly, it seemed, McGann got to his feet, his lined face clouded with anger he was just managing to control.

"It will be under the guise of bringing news to the paper, of course."

McGann nodded. He was thinking of Jillie.

"Enjoy the cigar, Tom." And he walked around the desk and saw McGann out the door.

Walking back to his desk he was thinking how sensible it was to know where the ghosts were in certain people's lives.

Outside in the street, Tom McGann was thinking of his daughter again; thankful that Jillie knew nothing about where the money had come from to send her east to college.

Then, as he stepped into the stirrup to mount his big chestnut stud horse, he let it all go. There was the work at hand. It was that that was important. Getting the beeves bunched and built into a herd, and then started. Then with his men positioned against any unexpected trouble, or in case of retaliation from the basin outfits, he'd have it all ready. Ready for the coming dawn. The other stockmen had fallen in with the idea just as easy as picking apples; and their loyalty was unquestioned.

But he would keep his eye on that sniveling son-ofabitch. Why Landusky wanted him in on things, he'd no idea, excepting maybe to keep a eye on him. But he had sure not liked the way he'd seen the bastard

looking at Jillie. If that happened again, to hell with
Landusky. He'd bust the little shit right now. And
Landusky, damn him, could tell the world whatever
he liked. But no, no, he couldn't. He'd put up with
it. He had to. He just had to. It would all be settled
soon. And he'd be shut of the Kid, and shut of Landusky too.

He looked at the sky, studying the clouds, the light.
Should be fair enough on the morrow. He sniffed,
spat down past his saddle scabbard. Tomorrow. Good
enough. He lifted his hat and resettled it on his graying
head. Suddenly he felt good. He was looking forward
to the action. And as he rode toward Hardwater Basin
he thought of Miriam. He still missed her. He supposed he always would. She'd been a good wife, by
God. A damn good wife. It was lonesome as hell
without her.

Then, his eye caught by an eagle soaring into the
limitless blue sky, he thought of the woman who had
set up in Crazy Woman Basin. He'd had her once
now. Lil, she said her name was. By God, when this
here was done with he'd go have some more of it.

11

At the Quarter Circle 22 spread it was quiet. As dusk fell and the lamps were lighted in the Kitchens' cabin, the three Kitchen brothers sat around the plank table with coffee and listened to John Slocum tell how he saw the situation.

"I see you're ready to fight, and I see that you're a bunch I certainly wouldn't want to mess with, but I have to tell you I don't agree with throwing up a wall of cattle when McGann and those others start pushing their beeves through."

"But it's the only thing we can do," Dusty Kitchen insisted. "They'll take our beeves if they can anyway, or butcher 'em. Hell, they've done it before. And they might even stampede their own cattle through here."

"I know that," Slocum said. "And I have seen the fence you've strung up, but that won't stop 'em. I know you're figuring on delay so's you'll be able to fire into them; if that's what you're aiming to do."

"We're gonna try an' stampede them, but going the other way," Dusty Kitchen said. "From our side."

"Might," Slocum said, squinting against the smoke from his quirly, which hung from the corner of his mouth. "Might be you could slow them, but you'll still have to square off. They'll outnumber you. Like that, you don't have a chance."

"Shit!" Jake Kitchen shook his head fast several times, as if chasing a fly. He was scowling. "What the hell kin we do then? Can't fight 'em square on, and can't fight 'em by running. Hell take it! I say we be wasting time settin' here jawin' about it. Let's get ourselves moving."

At this point a silence fell upon the group, while each of the Kitchens appeared to be deep in thought. Slocum had been waiting for the right moment to spring his idea; and now seemed as good a time as any.

"How do you see it, Slocum?" Dusty Kitchen said suddenly. "I got a feelin' you don't agree at all the way we got it figgered."

"It ain't the way I'd do her," Slocum said. "I just told you."

"How? How do you mean? How would you do it?" Sonny Kitchen asked, speaking for the first time.

"I don't see you putting up any more fence, or trying to shoot it out with them."

"What the hell do you want us to do?" Jake Kitchen demanded. "Just let 'em through? Let them have what they want? Shit!"

"They'll be expecting you to defend your homes, and go down fighting."

"But for sure!" the three Kitchens said in unison. "What the hell would a man do, but defend his home!

And we know we're going to lose our homes," Dusty said. "It's why we've sent the women up to Billings. But we ain't gonna give in without a fight!"

"What I am saying," Slocum said patiently, "is that you've got to figure something else instead of just playing into their hands by doing what they expect you to do."

"But how? How so?" Jake demanded. "What can we do? We've thought of every goddam possibility, and there just ain't no way out 'ceptin' to go down taking as many of the sonsofbitches with us as we can. The other outfits are going to do the same."

A silence fell suddenly then; and the three Kitchens turned their attention to Slocum, who was sitting quietly smoking his quirly.

He let a moment pass and when he spoke, he spoke quietly, and with conviction. At first he swiftly outlined their situation so that they'd all see the same thing together, as he put it.

"All you're doing then is setting yourselves up as targets for McGann and the others; you're doing what they expect you to do."

"But that's all there is; what else!" said Jake Kitchen.

"What I suggest you do is nothing," Slocum said quietly.

"Nothing!"

"Let them come through. You're outnumbered, outgunned, so you've finally seen you can't beat 'em, so you'll join them."

"Like hell we will!" said Jake furiously. "What the hell—"

"Shut up!" said Slocum. "And listen for a change. Dammit, you asked me, so now shut up and listen!"

He started to get up, ready to leave, but Dusty grabbed his arm.

"We're listening, Slocum. Come on now. And Jake, you be quiet, God dammit!" Dusty glared at his feisty brother, and then stared at Sonny to see if that young man was going to cause trouble. But Sonny was still, with his eyes on Slocum, and obviously listening.

Slocum leaned back in his chair, while Jake, still angry, nodded at him to go ahead.

"You've got all your cattle up by the tableland. Is that right?"

"Ourn' and the other outfits' too. They're all more or less together, if that's what you're askin'," Dusty said.

"Now look here." Slocum picked up a piece of paper and a pencil that were lying near his hand and began drawing.

"This is the tableland," he said. "And this is where your herds are. That right?"

"Right." It was Jake who was interested now. "What you gettin' at?"

"And this here is the butte, and there is the creek." He swiftly sketched as he talked. "Now then, I want you to get all your cattle out of where they are now. Push them up by the tableland. Here." He drew an indication of a big herd of cattle, making some concentric circles on the paper. Now then . . ." He leaned back, but with his hands still on the map. "Here is where the McGann herds will be coming—up through this gap. And you're going to have all your cattle at these two places. One bunch here, and the other over here."

He looked up from his design. "When the McGann steers get here"—he tapped the paper to show just where he meant—"then you'll start one of your herds down that draw, followed almost right away by the other, but coming in at a different angle." He indicated what he meant with little penciled marks on the paper. "See, they'll be coming through this here neck in the cut there dividing the tableland. And so you can stampede their herd with your cattle."

"That's gonna make one helluva mess," Sonny said, wagging his head in awe.

"That is just the point," Slocum said. "They won't expect you to stampede your own herd."

"A lot of beef is gonna get busted up," Dusty Kitchen said, grumbling. "It'll be one helluva mess."

"It'll be more of a mess if they get their cattle through without you making it as tough for them as you can. I think you've got a damn good chance of pulling it off."

They fell silent for some moments, taking in what Slocum had suggested. But then Dusty Kitchen pointed out that the McGann forces could stampede the whole shebang the other way, once they shot down a few of the small stockmen's herd; and since they had more men, a good many more than the small ranchers, they had the advantage in firepower and could simply overwhelm anything the small men might try.

"But I thought of that," Slocum said. "That's why I brought that box that's now lying in your chuck wagon. Dunno if you noticed."

"Box?" Jake asked. "What you got in there— some new automatic weapon, I'll be bound."

But Slocum was shaking his head. "What I've got is a box full of some smaller, more accurate weapons." He paused. "I want you to understand very well what I am telling you. You will some of you use rifles, but the rest of you will use those sticks of dynamite, and you bust that herd, and the men driving those poor critters." He shook his head. "I hate to destroy those cattle, but it's them or yourselves and your families." And he looked calmly into the gray faces of the Kitchens.

"You've got it clear now? You won't be here when they come. The place will be deserted. They'll simply figure you've pulled up stakes. But they came here pretty sure you were going to dig in and fight for your ground. So, they'll be thrown some; for the moment. They'll let down their guard, see. If it goes like that you can start picking some of them off. You'll be up here in those rimrocks." He pointed with the pencil at the map again. "Or even if you don't, even if you just wait, they'll be pushing through anyway and they'll come right through this cut here. If they see you, or if you decide to pick some of them off and they come after you, retreat. Just keep retreating till you get them in that narrow cut there." He tapped the piece of paper again. "Maybe you even let them see one of you, and so they'll follow. You decoy them. And when they're here in the cut, you let them have it."

"Stampede the cattle," Sonny said in a hoarse voice.

Slocum nodded. "That is the size of it." He stood up.

"With the dynamite. Let's get going."

It was all over by the middle of the next forenoon. The McGann forces had clearly been overconfident, as Slocum had suspected they would be. The Kitchens and some of their allies had retreated into the rimrocks where the cattle were being held. And the McGann crowd had pursued. Slocum had recognized some of the faces; and he'd identified—from earlier description—their immediate field leader Use Moriarty. Two of the Kitchen crowd had been winged, though the three brothers hadn't even been scratched, and a couple of McGann's men had been wounded. No dead. And it had been a victory for the Kitchens and their neighbors in and around Hardwater Basin.

Yet it was for Slocum unsatisfactory. For nothing had really been decided. The big stockmen had been repulsed, but it was as though their principal leaders, their important men, hadn't bothered to attend what they must have considered—from the comfort and safety of their leather armchairs in the Cheyenne Club where they jostled and discussed with none other than their own kind—a small battle in a larger scheme of things. At any rate, that was the definite feeling that Slocum brought with him from the field of battle.

Of course, the Kitchens were exultant; and his cautioning them not to let their guards down was hardly heard. Even his reminder that obviously McGann and his men were playing the same game the Hardwater bunch had played—retreating only to get the other one off guard—fell on deaf ears. Although by the time Slocum saddled up the Appaloosa and got ready to ride into Landusky, Dusty Kitchen had started to hear what he was saying.

"I got the notion, Dusty, that the fight's really going on someplace else. Not that it means you won't be affected here in the basin. But you understand, some fights are settled before a shot is fired, even though the firing takes place; and some are settled after."

"And you're figuring the fight's taking place in town."

Slocum, with his hand holding rein and some of the Appaloosa's mane, and about to step into his stirrup, nodded. "Tell me where the Kid was. And McGann. Moriarty was running the show. But where were those two, and who knows who else that's important in the setup."

"And you're going to be looking for some of it in town?" Dusty Kitchen pushed his hat onto the back of his head. He was listening seriously to Slocum, but yet could not hide his elation at what he and the others considered a great victory.

Slocum swung up and over, settling down into his old, beat-up stock saddle. He looked down at Dusty Kitchen, his eyes shaded by the wide brim of his black Stetson hat. He hadn't answered Dusty's question, but now he did.

"I got me a notion that it'll unravel pretty directly once I get to town. Like I figure somebody is looking for me." And he nodded and kicked the Appaloosa into a fast walk, which in a moment or so broke into a canter.

Dusty Kitchen stood where they had both been talking and watched him ride away. When his brother Sonny came up and stood beside him neither of them spoke. They just stood there watching Slocum ride out of sight.

"Reckon he'll be back?" Jake asked, coming up to them.

Dusty Kitchen leaned over and pressed his thumb against the side of his nose and blew. He straightened up, sniffing. "Dunno."

"Jeez," said Sonny Kitchen. "I sure hope so."

Neither of his brothers said anything to that. And the three continued to stand where they were even after Slocum had ridden out of their sight.

• • •

With all the restrained excitement of the quickening range war there were some people in Landusky who forgot that this day happened to be the Fourth of July. Miles Landusky, for whom the town had been named, was one.

The editor of the *Declaimer* was always happy to forget the "Glorious Fourth," not because he was unpatriotic—quite the reverse; like many who challenged society he believed thoroughly in the cardinal virtues—but because the noise reminded him too immediately of his unfortunate accident in the express car with the dynamite explosion. The result being, he somehow refused to accept even the possibility of sudden and explosive noise. On the Fourth he generally kept close to himself, even "forgetting" that the Great Celebration existed.

And so on the day of the confrontation that proved such a dud at Hardwater Basin, he was sitting comfortably at his desk going over his ledgers and congratulating himself on the neat way things were coming his way. When suddenly the door of his office opened and someone walked in without knocking.

A long moment of silence followed the appearance of this person who stood still, with the door now closed behind him; and the two men regarded each other without moving or speaking. From outside came the sound of firecrackers celebrating the Fourth.

Finally, Miles Landusky took the matter in hand, saying, "Sir, what can I do for you?"

"Hello, Butch."

"There is nobody here by that name, sir. I believe you've made a mistake and are in the wrong place." As he said those words, Landusky's hand opened the desk drawer right in front of him.

And in less than a breath there was the big six-gun in the visitor's fist. "Don't try it!"

"Try what, sir? I was simply looking for a cigar. And why are you pointing that gun at me?"

"Come off that line, Butch. I spotted you easy."

"You have the advantage of me, sir. I suppose I'll have to humor you. You have obviously mistaken me for somebody else."

The Kid was grinning. He sniffed. Landusky was looking for the drop of water that he had seen so often at the tip of that long, pale, skinny nose; but it wasn't there.

"What do you want—money?"

"I'll take that gun, Butch. Hand it over carefully."

"Of course, sir. Only there isn't any gun in this drawer."

"By the way, Butch, I was out at Hardwater Basin, and McGann and his bunch got nowhere. See, I just thought I'd report in—to the great newspaperman. I been hearing about all your writings all over the place, Butch. Shows what a education can do for you, don't it?"

"You're making a very big mistake, mister. You've got me mixed up with somebody else."

"Cut it out, Butch. Now, just hand over that gun."

"But . . . there isn't any gun in this drawer."

"Hand it over!"

"But I can't. Take a look. There's no gun there! I'm telling you the truth, dammit!" He raised his fist to cough into it. "Take a look for yourself. Look, I'll stand back and you can see. I can't hand you something that isn't there!"

And for that moment he saw the Kid hesitate.

"All I wanted from the drawer was a cigar. I am telling you, mister, there is no gun in that drawer."

And he reached up and coughed nervously again into his fist. Then he held his hands up, wide, and said, "Look, I only wanted a cigar. You want one? I have them sent from Frisco." And the smile that he chose to go with those words was placating, even warm, bordering just a little on the servile. Though of course the Kid wouldn't see it. Nobody ever saw his smile, or anything else for that matter.

Suddenly he watched the Kid's eyes drop to the cigar box on the desk.

"Whyn't you take a cigar from that box?"

"The ones in the drawer are fresher," he said. "But very well, I'll take one of these. Want one?"

The Kid's eyes were like two oysters, he was thinking. And by God, there—there it was, right on the end of that long, bony nose; the drop of water! It flashed through his mind that this was something he just couldn't believe. But how the hell had he found him out!

"You're wondering how I figured it was you, huh—Butch." He grinned, that sickening, white grin, fishbelly white and damp. The laugh that followed was like a muted klaxon, reveling in its cleverness as well as its ability to annoy everyone. "It was easy. It was from seeing you from your back, Butch. See, you can change things by looking in a mirror and working at it; but you can't see yer back in a mirror."

"Do you want to look in this drawer to make sure I have no gun here? And then, perhaps you'd like to leave and look for whoever it is you're looking for someplace else."

He had made his tone firm, but not threatening; more on the order of parent or schoolteacher. He had studied some of the Kid's weak spots in the old days. "Anyway, my boy, I've a lot of work to do and you'll have to excuse me. Would you please examine this drawer, or anything else you want to in the room, and then excuse me.'' He made a cold smile to finish all those words. ''And, if you don't mind, I would like a cigar. I offer you one. They're sent me from San Francisco. Pure Havana tobacco. A real treat.''

And before the Kid could say yes or no, he had reached to the humidor box on his desk, opened the lid, and brought out two cigars. ''Have one?''

He dropped a cigar onto the edge of the desk in front of the Kid, retaining the other for himself.

The Kid was watching him with loaded eyes, and with that silly smile on his face for which he was famous.

''The drive through the Kitchen place was a wash-out, Butch. I don't reckon you've heard yet. I really cut my little pinto hoss to get in here and be the first to get the news to you!'' His grin was wide, pale, wet looking, like some kind of fish sucking air. Landusky looked at him with loathing, secure in the knowledge that behind his mask nobody could tell what was going on.

''Excuse me,'' Landusky said, and picked up a paper on his desk to look at it.

The Kid stood motionless in front of him with the gun still in his hand. Yet, there was not the same tension that had been there at the beginning.

Landusky laid the paper down on the desk carefully, and then, suddenly catching himself as he spotted the still-open humidor box in a direct line between himself and the Kid, he shook his head in a scolding gesture. ''Stupid! I keep leaving it open and of course that means the cigars will dry out. Anyway, we also need a light.'' And his hand reached out to shut the lid of the cigar humidor.

"It's a handly little humidor. I got it in Italy."

And in that second in which he said the word "Italy," his hand, hidden by the open lid, darted into the box and came up with the derringer and he shot the Kid right in the throat. The Kid's finger pulled the trigger of his own gun and the bullet smashed into the wall behind Butch Killigan's head.

The six-gun fell from the Kid's dying hand, his eyes stared in a great bulge as though they belonged to a giant fish, and he sank to the floor and lay there in his mass of ill-fitting clothes.

Butch Killigan stood looking down at the dying man on the floor of his office. "Thanks for the tip about my back," he said. "I will learn something from that. But you, Kid, you still don't learn. Remember how many times I used to tell you, 'Never trust an unarmed man'?"

He ejected the shell from the derringer, reloaded it, and placed it carefully in the humidor box. Then he pulled open the desk drawer, took out two cigars, and placed them in the empty space in the box where he had removed the other two from the row. The derringer was now neatly covered again. He closed the lid, arranged the box so that it was in the precise position in which he wanted it.

Then he looked down at the Kid. The Kid was dead. He knew from McGann that the Kid had wanted a shot at John Slocum. Well, maybe Butch Killigan— as the Kid's leader—would have to see that the job was done. After all, there was such a thing as finishing a job that had been started, even if only by an underling. A sort of question of honor.

All morning the firecrackers had been popping, children had been taking over the day throwing the crackers about, scaring one another and irritating their parents. For even though it was the Fourth—the day of celebration—there was something missing in the town. It was more like an expectation of something not good, even a foreboding.

Thus far there had been no disturbance in town. The action, as far as any of the citizens knew, was taking place out at Hardwater Basin. But gradually certain pieces of news began to drift into town and added to the kind of heaviness that pervaded the streets, the stores, the houses. Only occasional laughter could be heard, and this from the children.

John Slocum had picked up on the town's tight gloom the moment he rode in. Some heads turned to watch him, but not too openly. There were questions in the faces. He rode right up to the Elkhorn, dismounted, wrapped his reins loosely around the hitch rail, and then pushed in through the batwing doors.

It was cool, dark in the deep interior. The patrons were not many, but this was not unusual for the time of day. He knew the place would begin to fill up soon enough.

Cornelius was behind the bar, standing there with arms akimbo watching Slocum approach.

Neither man said anything as the bartender placed a bottle and glass on the bar.

"Heard about the McGann bunch being drove back with the beeves an' dynamite and all," Cornelius said. "How's it goin' now; you hear anythin'?"

"They pushed 'em outta there; the Kitchens and the others. I believe McGann and them will leave them be, for a spell anyways. And maybe something can be worked out."

"But McGann had to back off," Cornelius said. "That's the way of it I heerd."

Slocum nodded. "Yup. Both sides lost a lot of cattle. Couple men took lead, but nobody died of it."

Some men came through the swinging doors then, and Slocum watched them in the mirror. Cowpokes, but he didn't think they'd been at the ruckus out in Hardwater.

Cornelius returned after serving them at the other end of the bar. He leaned forward confidentially, his enormous belly bulging over the mahogany.

"You know that feller—the Kid?"

Slocum nodded. "I had a notion he was looking for me, so I rode in just to see what's doing."

Cornelius's huge bronze eyes were almost out of their sockets as he leaned even further forward, and he was clearly short of breath. "Somebody shot him."

"Dead?"

"He is dead—dead."

"Hunh." Slocum lifted his glass and took a swallow. "Who did it? Was he bushwhacked?"

"Not bushwhacked. Shot right in the throat and died. The body was found out in the street, south side of town. Looks like somebody outdrew him, or leastways scored first."

"No sign of anyone else around?" Slocum asked. "Blood or anything?"

"Marshal figured he was shot someplace else and then drug into the alley where some kids playing with the fireworks found him."

"Hunh."

"What you think?" Cornelius leaned back a little, releasing the strain on his big belly.

"What do I think?" Slocum looked in the mirror to see if anyone else had come in. Two men were just entering. "I think it looks like somebody was faster and surer than the Kid," he said.

Now, seeing another man enter and move to the side of the room, he looked at Cornelius.

"We have got company," he said. "You know about it?"

The bartender's long, flat cheeks were the color of chalk. "Slocum, I don't know a thing. But I don't want them wrecking the place. You reckon they be lookin' for you?"

"I don't think they're looking for George Washington."

"You want to go outside, Slocum? I don't want this place all shot up."

Slocum lifted his glass, drained it. He nodded as he put the empty down on the bar. "Thanks for the hospitality," he said, and saw two more men enter, making a total of five new arrivals in the past few minutes.

As he started toward the batwing doors he wondered whether McGann was around, and what he would find outside. What he found on the boardwalk was Marshal Luther Bones and his deputy.

"I am arrestin' you, Slocum. Hand over yer gun."

"What for?" Out of the side of his eye he saw a young boy who was about to run by them suddenly stop and stare. He was holding a sparkler firecracker, while nearby another firecracker went off.

"For disturbing the peace. I'm talking about up at Hardwater Basin. Incitin' people and stampeding cattle; and where'n hell did you get that dynamite?"

Slocum suddenly saw the big man with the damaged face coming toward them. He had crossed the street and now stepped up onto the boardwalk.

"What's the trouble, Marshal?"

"No trouble, Mr. Landusky. Just arresting this man for disturbances out at Hardwater Basin, and also some unfinished business when he was in jail before and got out on agreement he'd be helping Tom McGann with his cattle drive to the summer graze. But from what I have heard, he just took off. And also he is packing a gun, which he ain't s'posed to be doin'."

Landusky stood facing Slocum now. "That right, Slocum?"

Slocum had taken out a wooden lucifer while the marshal was talking and now put it in his mouth, holding it there like a toothpick. Then he shifted his position so that he was not standing with the sun in his eyes. All at once he spotted a figure moving on a roof across the street.

"Well, maybe Mr. Slocum and I can have a talk and get the straight of things," Landusky said. "I have heard a number of things about you, Slocum. Most of them good; but I'd like to hear your side of it."

Slocum didn't move. "There isn't any side to it, Landusky. There is what happened. These gents along with McGann tried to ramrod me. Except that ain't your business anyway. Or is it?"

"I do believe it is."

"Let's see what they think," Slocum said as he nodded at the horsemen coming up the street behind Landusky and the two lawmen.

The riders were eight: three Kitchens, Tom McGann, and four men Slocum had seen out at Hardwater who he presumed were with the Kitchens.

It was McGann who spoke first. "Landusky, I heard what happened. I mean about that little sonofabitch you foisted on me—"

"Shut up!" snapped Landusky, his face turning

red, almost scarlet. "You damn fool, keep your mouth shut!"

But McGann wasn't giving ground. "I'm through, Landusky. You understand me? You hear me!"

"Moriarty!" Landusky brought the name out like a whip cracking into the startled street.

A man Slocum did not know stepped away from the crowd that had gathered right outside the saloon. He was tall, lean. His hand was a blur, and so was the gun as he drew, raised it, and smashed it across McGann's face, knocking him to the boardwalk.

A gasp rose from the group watching.

Slocum didn't hesitate. His gun was out and he slammed it against Use Moriarty's gun arm. The weapon that had smashed McGann fell useless into the street.

And suddenly the crowd had dispersed. Some diving for cover. Others, who were obviously in on the play, took up positions from where they might be most effective in any ensuing combat.

Use Moriarty was holding his forearm, grimacing with pain. A string of curses fell from his mouth, all sounding like one word in the stream of rage.

Slocum saw the movement of Landusky's hand, caught the sunflash on the gun barrel on the roof across the street, and dove away. He was in the street, rolling in the dust, and then up and had fired, hitting the rifleman on the roof.

"Slocum!"

It was Marshal Bones throwing down on him now. "You are under arrest. Throw down that gun."

"Just a minute, Bones."

And this time the voice was Tom McGann's. "I've got you covered right between the shoulder blades."

By now the street was about deserted, except for the principals outside the Elkhorn.

"You're talking to the law, McGann," snapped Bones, hopping to turn around so he could face the rancher.

But McGann held his gun steady. "You are talking about Miles Landusky's law, Bones. And I am telling you and Landusky and everybody in this town that I've had enough of it. I am through. Landusky, you tell these people any goddam thing you like, you son-ofabitch!"

Suddenly a shot rang out and McGann staggered, dropped his gun as he clutched at his arm. It was Deputy Wall who had fired. All attention was on this special tableau now as Wall faced the rancher. "You be under arrest, mister," the deputy said.

At which point something told Slocum to watch it. Out of the side of his eye he saw Landusky's hand slip toward the gun at his hip.

"Slocum!"

They were facing each other and Landusky had already started for his gun. But suddenly his hand shifted and sped for the belly gun concealed under his shirt.

Slocum's hand whistled to the Colt. There was the sound of only one shot.

The hideout fell from Landusky's hand, while the man stood there, as though suddenly frozen, and then he tumbled to the street.

"Goddlemighty!" Somebody gasped the word.

Deputy Wall started to move, but McGann, re-covered from the surprise and pain of his shoulder wound, had him covered.

Slocum stood looking down at the dying man, who had managed to roll onto his back.

Miles Landusky stared up dimly at the man standing over him. "Jesus . . . Never knew there was anybody faster'n . . . faster'n . . ."

He was choking.

"Faster than Butch Killigan?"

A murmur touched the small group that had been a part of it.

The man in the street was trying to speak. Slocum hunkered down beside him.

"How'd you know I was—was . . . Butch?"

Slocum hesitated only a moment. "I read it in your paper—the *Declaimer*. You wrote in one of your stories about the famous outlaw who had a trick of pretending to draw his handgun, but then coming on with a hideout. You said in the story that he was known as Butch." He watched the man breathing very faintly. "It is hard to live down a reputation, I reckon. Sometimes you can hide the outside; but the inside, that's a horse of a different color."

Later, talking to the Kitchen brothers over a drink in the Elkhorn, he again refused their offer to have him settle in Hardwater Basin.

"I'm not the settling kind," he said.

"Good thing for us you ain't," Sonny said swiftly.

At which his two older brothers turned on him in total surprise. "Well by damn! That boy is sharp as this morning's rooster!"

And they all had a good laugh at that.

Much, much later, after they had spent time in bed, Jillie McGann asked him what was going to happen with her father.

"Nothing. He's come clean about everything. Landusky—or Killigan—was twisting him, and he had to do what he said; to protect you was how he saw it. You got a good man for a father, young lady.''

She reached down and squeezed him in a good place. "And I have got a really, really great lover. . . ."

"You'll have to prove that to me, young lady," Slocum said as he rolled over on top of her.